with the

Ashes

catching

Daybreak

with the
Ashes
catching
Daybreak

NELLY ALIKYAN

*To all those who will fight
for the love they've always wanted.*

ALSO BY NELLY ALIKYAN

Catchers Series

With the Flames Catching Midnight

With the Rains Catching Dawn

With the Ice Catching Twilight

With the Storms Catching Dusk

With the Winds Catching Sunlight

With the Ashes Catching Daybreak

Whittle Magic Series

Alluring Darkness

Beholding Darkness

Claiming Darkness

Desiring Darkness

ALSO BY N. ALIKYAN

Buttercup Baby

Promise of A Lifetime

CHAPTER 1
ATIANA

The audacity of that man. Sure, he ran the nation, but to think he would obligate Ashtyn, who was frankly doing him a favor by healing people from this plague, to marry.

King Edmund was a fair man, one who understood and took accountability for his past mistakes, now trying to right them. He looked over all the members of the Posse like they were all his children and never threatened any of the servants when they inevitably did part of their job incorrectly. If at times he seemed cruel, it was simply to keep things in line, never because he wanted to hurt another. He was just.

But to think he would force her to marry!

Atiana's eyes narrowed to such slits all she saw was Edmund on his horse, flashes of his sword swiping in. Nothing else. Not Gabriel on the other horse, the trees in the background, or the beauty of Absko as he worked with the King to win their duel.

Then Edmund stumbled, and his head shot toward her direction. His eyes were wide after landing on her like he couldn't fathom what he'd done wrong. The look almost shocked Atiana out of her anger—why would the King care if she was angry with him? Though a just man, he never paid particular interest to the petty problems the servants may have with him.

His brows furrowed, then he turned back into the training with Gabriel.

Atiana shook her head. If only she had the courage his daughters—which she'd just learned of the second when Princess Rosaelia said she trusted Atiana too much to keep Evony's blood from her—had to be so bold as to confront him about it.

"No." Ashtyn broke her out of her thoughts, reminding Atiana that they'd been speaking of her. "Not at all. They simply let me know that it will be the easier course to keep the men away. Everything, even showing my abilities to help with the plague, has been left to my decision."

Atiana sighed, her gaze softening on the man. That was the man she knew Edmund to be. "Well, we all know you will help them, so the question is—will you choose a husband?"

"I cannot imagine marrying anyone."

Atiana barely stopped herself from scoffing, wanting to show the serenity that allowed her friends to feel comfortable speaking to her about things they didn't tell others. So she quirked a brow instead. "No?"

"What's the supposed to mean? I just said no."

When was the poor girl going to stop fighting her attraction? "Ashtyn, be true to yourself."

"Wha—"

"Gabriel," Atiana interrupted.

It wasn't surprising to get an eye roll from the healer. "Do not worry about any relationship with Gabriel. We are... cordial. You are free to pursue him as you wish."

Atiana's eyes bugged out of her face as she coughed the shock away. "Are you out of your mind?" What could have possibly sent her to such ludicrous conclusions?

"Excuse m—"

"Why would I ever want Gabriel?"

"You are the one watching him. I've seen you two together."

Sadness passed through her. "Trust me. I have no interest in Gabriel. To me, he truly is a friend. To you, however, things are quite different. Everyone here knows you two are spoken for. Why else do you think none of the men have come for you, other than because of your charming personality, that is?"

"Then why are you—" Ashtyn cut herself off as her gaze landed back on the men.

Atiana fought off her blush. What did it matter if the healer realized her outrageous feelings for the King? The girl hated everyone at the palace. She surely wasn't going to add to the gossip mills. Not that Atiana much cared if she were added to the mills.

Then Ashtyn rolled her eyes in Atiana's direction. "Oh, you're so cliché."

"Me?" Atiana exclaimed. "Gabriel is the charming, sweet stablehand. It doesn't get more cliché than falling for him."

"It doesn't get more cliché than falling for the King? Really? That's your argument?"

Atiana's cheeks pinked now, then even more so as she realized the men were coming off their horses and approaching them. "Shut up," she hissed.

"Atiana," Gabriel called right on time to stop his healer from saying anything more. "Do not be angry with me. The big thing passing off as a horse ripped the shirt, I didn't!"

Atiana laughed as her gaze traveled from Gabriel over Edmund to Absko. The King's horse was her favorite, and she felt a little thrill when the horse neighed in her direction. "Hey! Don't be mean to Absko. He's a sweetheart."

Gabriel scoffed. "You only say that because he likes you. You and Ed. That's it."

As Atiana's cheeks pinked a little more at hearing anything between her and *Ed*, Ashtyn muttered under her breath, "Yeah because he knows who his owners are."

Atiana slammed her elbow into the healer before she said anything more, anything louder. "I think he can tell you have singled him out of all the horses as the one you do not like. You cannot treat poor Absko like that!"

She looked back at the horse, wanting to step up to him and pet his mane, but refraining because of the King's proximity. Then her gaze subconsciously landed on said King.

He was so handsome, even with the hard look he wore around her. It was affirming enough to know he didn't treat any of the help particularly friendly, but it stung to constantly get such a cold stare when all she'd wanted for nearly seven years was one of those stunning smiles he kept exclusively for his Posse.

"I have not singled anyone out," Gabriel exclaimed, thankfully breaking Atiana's stare. "He singled himself out by being mean to everyone but you two."

When Atiana's gaze landed on the stable hand, his smile was so infectious, she couldn't help but return it.

"I'm sure he'll treat you well enough when you're feeding him too many treats," the King finally said, his voice brooding, sending shivers straight down Atiana's spine. "I should be heading inside."

He passed the reins to Gabriel right as Ashtyn exclaimed, "Perfect!" Then as the King walked toward them to get to the palace, Ashtyn quickly placed Atiana's hand in the crook of his elbow. "Atiana was just saying she needed to get back to work. Why don't you walk her to her suite?"

Atiana swallowed, frozen in the moment. She was touching him. Yes, it was over his finely-sourced jacket that Odolf had made, but she'd never touched him.

It only took a couple seconds to snap herself out of the shock as her gaze jumped up to the cold dark orbs of the King, and she began to pull her hand away. She wasn't a violent woman, but Ashtyn might be made the exception.

Then the unexpected happened, and the King tucked his arm into his side so her hand was stuck there. "Very well."

His voice was soothing and tempting all at once, almost like he was making a promise with his words. Or maybe breaking a promise.

Atiana didn't get the chance to respond as Edmund turned them for the palace. Her free hand at her side jittered. It was the only source of release for all the nerves racing through her body.

She felt the gazes of everyone as they moved through the greens, into the palace, and toward the tailor's wing where her suite was. She didn't care. They could talk all they'd like. Those would be true rumors for the gossip mills, ones that held no merit as the King hadn't spoken a word to her the entire time. Those rumors would be based on no facts. Though even if rumors based on fact spread, she wouldn't care as long as they were reciprocated ones.

Her hand was at the crook of his elbow but she felt the muscle of his bicep still. It was solid. His side, where her hand was tucked into, was also solid. She imagined all of him was solid. Unsurprisingly considering he trained with his men daily.

Her periphery took in his profile. He didn't wear his emotions on his sleeve, a positive for a king, but obstructive to her goals of reading him a little. From what she could tell though, he looked angry. His eyes were as cold as ever, and she swore there was a grimace about his lips.

She swallowed the shot of rejection that rushed through her limbs and blinked rapidly to lose any wateriness that presented itself. There was no reason to assume his disapproval was to do with her, but she couldn't help remembering any moment between them, all of the small rejections of her. How his lips would thin every time she offered to do his tailoring.

They were nearly at her suite, the corridors in the tailor's wing empty as most were off doing other things at this hour. Atiana made herself keep her focus on her door only a few yards out, knowing this was close to ending. She didn't want it to, it was her only chance to ever touch him, but she needed to be away from him before the sting of his disgust with her cut any deeper.

They stopped in front of her door and as she tugged on her hand, he didn't release it. His arm was tucked so tightly into his body, she couldn't move.

"Your Highness," she whispered as that was all the energy she could put into the words and tugged on her hand once more, her other hand on the handle to her door.

His dark orbs caught hers and he held her stare, almost like he was challenging her. When her brows furrowed, he finally released her.

She swallowed as she slowly removed her hand from his arm and turned her back on him. When she entered her room, door safely closed, she rested her back on it. Her eyes watered, but she didn't have tears. It was difficult to have tears because tears meant a hope was broken. She'd never had any hope of his feelings for her being favorable.

She took a large breath in, and as she pushed off her door, a hard knock slammed into it. A large fist capable of breaking down the door altogether.

Her brows furrowed as she opened it to find the King on the other side. "Your Highness?"

He rushed inside, slamming the door behind him as his hands cradled her face, breath hitting her face. "Don't call me that, Atiana. Please."

His lips crashed into hers before she could make out what was happening.

EDMUND

Sparrow was stretching on the mats of the Posse's private training room when Edmund arrived early in the morning. They had a standing meeting to train on days he planned on being too busy to join his guards and being that Sparrow was the Master Assassin, fighting him was the best training any man could get. As long as their ego didn't get hurt at the fact that the man couldn't be beat.

Edmund joined him in the middle of the mats, neither speaking as they stretched side by side. Then Sparrow opened, "The babe was kicking up a storm in Evony's belly this morning. I don't think he wanted me to leave."

Edmund smiled. "Have you two started talking of names? There're only a few more months before my first grandheir is here."

"She decided long ago that a boy would be named after my father. We haven't spoken about it much for a girl. She says we won't know until we see her."

Edmund shook his head. "Ah, that girl. She's had control over you since she arrived."

Sparrow winked as he moved for the side table with all sorts of weapons lined on it to take his pick. He normally chose the heaviest one to balance out the power between himself and his opponent. "You're in a good mood this morning, Ed."

"My grandbaby is kicking. Is that nothing to be joyous over?"

Sparrow smirked. "Very much so. Except your joy was permeating before I said that."

Edmund took his choice of sword and stopped in the middle of the mats once more. "Don't analyze me, Sparrow."

"You know, there's a lot of talk that you walked Atiana to her suite yesterday. Lots of questions on why you would do such a thing."

Edmund ignored the way his adopted son tried to goad him into admitting anything and played offense in their duel. Their swords met with loud slams but they were both eloquent as they moved on the mats.

"The general rumor would be something is happening, especially given she is the most beautiful woman at this palace, but given she's been here for years and you haven't been seen together, they're coming up with other theories."

"Fascinating," Edmund muttered as he focused on the swords in order to refrain from thinking about walking Atiana to her room yesterday. In order to forget that he'd lost control of himself and kissed her. He'd spent the whole of the night obsessing over it, dreaming of it. It'd been the best sleep of his life.

"I believe the most popular theory so far is that you two are conspiring for a surprise for Odolf as the man is getting older now," Sparrow continued. "My guess was that you two must be speaking of the matters for Ashtyn's trip."

Edmund huffed. "Since when do you gossip, Sparrow?"

The Assassin smirked, slamming his sword against

Edmund's and knocking them both to the side. "I'm not gossiping. My theory has been spoken to my wife alone. But I know that's not what it was."

Edmund didn't entertain him with responses, using more energy to fight him off to keep the memory of Atiana's tongue intertwined with his out of his mind.

"We both know my rebellious little wife. She had to know *something*." Sparrow worked him harder, silencing both of them for a couple of minutes as they traveled around the mats and when their swords slammed together and froze, he finished by saying, "So she sent her magic into your mind for a quick moment."

Edmund froze, the power in his arm pushing against Sparrow's a little more than before. "What?"

Sparrow wore a shining grin now, as mischievous as his wife's. "Our question now is whether you were imagining kissing her or remembering it?"

Edmund broke their swords contact, then thrust again. They moved around the mats another minute before he needed the break. But all the while, he raged over his daughter's actions.

They moved in frightening synchrony for some time before Edmund could no longer take the strain of such a fight with the Master Assassin, and he dropped his sword to indicate a break. He was only thankful Sparrow hadn't tried to converse in all that time. He'd needed it to push away his anger at his daughter—though she deserved to act out against him after everything he'd put her through—and to especially push back those very vivid memories of Atiana.

As he was getting his water, Sparrow stopped beside him, more serious now. "Don't be angry with Evony. She wasn't trying to violate you. She was planning on bringing us into your mind to speak to you but then we saw that and realized you probably wouldn't be open to speaking."

"Us?" Edmund demanded.

He shrugged. "She can connect multiple minds. There was no need to relay information if I could simply be there."

Edmund took a final pull of his water before stopping on the mats once more. "Let's go again. I have meetings today and I'd rather feel the pain of my body than suffer through them fully aware."

Sparrow laughed as he joined him, both readying into position. His eyes twinkled in a way that only started a few months ago. After meeting Evony. "So, a memory then?"

Edmund met his second's gaze, both men's brown orbs twinkling. A memory, yes, but he didn't need to know that. "I understand you feel a need to know everything, Assassin, but mind your business."

Sparrow smirked. "As you wish, *Your Highness.*"

Edmund attacked as his son laughed.

OUTSIDE OF THE POSSE, Edmund needed to trust one other group with certainty. They were hand-picked by himself and the three men of his Posse. Sparrow, Miels, and Tristan had been instrumental in weeding out anyone who somehow convinced Edmund they were there without ill intent.

The group was put together for the sole purpose of breaking down the laws his father had made years ago, ones he'd carried on until a few years ago when he'd decided it was time to allow magicians, and possibly sorcerers, back on the lands. Sorcerers were a more difficult feat considering they were solely on the Island, and Islanders on their own were dangerous, not to mention any with extra power. So that was on hold at the moment.

Though having Islanders in his Posse now, his son-in-law being one, meant when they did begin to slowly open borders, they would have insight that wouldn't have been possible without Killian, Norya, and the nonas.

But this group was focused on magicians at the moment. Given all magicians lived in the Southern Lands, things were easier. The first of all being that the border between the North and South was open so they didn't have to worry about the peoples clashing. They already traversed back and forth.

Edmund had also made sure none of his Posse were in this group. That way he could get full insight before taking it to them—because nothing would be decided without all of them agreeing on the matter. And now he was even happier about that decision because his Posse was so much bigger than it had been before and he needed a solid plan before presenting it to them, before presenting it to his daughter—the Master Magician.

"The travels around the Northern Lands were a beauty," Aliyev, his manager for this endeavor, remarked. "Catalina especially loved the opportunity to visit each village."

Edmund smirked. "I'm sure your wife is very thankful you love her dearly enough to fight me on bringing her along." He normally wouldn't have allowed for spouses to go together because Catalina's presence would slow down the trip. The only reason Edmund had ended up allowing it was because Aliyev insisted, and the man never asked for anything.

He smirked. "She was mighty thankful."

Edmund quirked a brow. In the Northern Lands, there was a level of propriety that the other lands didn't hold to. Aliyev wouldn't speak on his activities with his wife, but the way his eyes shined as he remembered the trip, Edmund knew Catalina had rewarded her husband thoroughly.

Vardan cleared his throat. "And your findings?"

Aliyev's eyes cleared of emotion as he turned back to the matter at hand. "As expected, I'm afraid. There were a few curious bodies, especially down by the borders, but most were more frightful of what may come with magicians."

Aliyev's mission had been a simple one. Travel around the north—and with his wife along, they could make it out as a honeymoon for their ten-year anniversary—and ask patrons what they thought of magicians and how they might feel if one was living by them. Aliyev had trained with Tristan and Sparrow before heading out, so Edmund knew he would've been able to wedge the topic into any conversation he was having, especially with his wife around to help him.

Asha shrugged, her hair tied back in a loose bun to keep herself from playing nervously with it. "We expected such. Were you able to find out anything that may help them see magicians as good?"

Asha and Yarro had been the two sent down to the Southern Lands when Edmund decided once and for all that he wanted the reinstatement of magicians to happen at the start of the new year. That was mere weeks away, so the two had been tasked with learning what they could about magicians— whether they'd like to live up here, what they may need to feel safe doing so, and more.

Asha didn't admit to it, but she ended up falling for the brother of one of the magicians she'd spoken with. Yarro wasn't a gossip, but he'd told them that much.

"Most were simply afraid. The older ones hardly remember a time with magicians so they cannot accurately remember whether they were harmful or not, and the younger have never been around them. I think having magicians around to show them that they are not bad would help ease them into it," Aliyev stated.

"Good," Edmund huffed. "I have my healer and her husband going to the Southern Lands soon. I will have them look for magicians to bring back with them. I think it'll be especially helpful to the Northern public if they see these magicians helping stop the plague."

They all nodded, but it was Yarro who finally spoke, "In that case, I believe some gossip shall begin passing. We do not want a sudden appearance of magicians, but we also don't want such gossip as to lead to hysteria."

"What would you suggest?" Edmund asked.

"We may begin with passing gossip around the palace. Only a few people need to hear us discussing it 'in private' in the halls for the news to spread. It is more likely that the news will hit the neighboring towns and the Southern border far sooner than the Northern side. The more accepting those by the border and around here are, the easier it'll be to convince those farther up north that the magicians mean no harm."

"Good. Then let's not think too deeply on it. No need to overcomplicate this," Edmund finalized.

Vardan smirked, getting to his feet. "Yarro, would you like to take a walk to the kitchens?"

They all chuckled as Yarro answered, "Love to."

Everyone knew some of the worst gossips spent their time by the kitchens where they knew everyone passed by at some point. It was the best spot to secure such juicy news.

CHAPTER 3

EDMUND

Edmund made his way through the remaining of his meetings, but after dealing with the magician problem, it was difficult to keep his mind off of certain matters for too long.

His suite, in instances like these, was a haven. It situated his common sitting space, his bedroom, and his office all in one. It was dark, normally with the curtains drawn to keep the sun out, and probably didn't help his moodiness. He felt comforted by it.

Comforted but never fully at home. He didn't want anyone to change the way his place looked. Not anyone.

But her.

Edmund readied himself a cup of tea and took it to his office. Leaning off to the side of the room was the portrait they'd found at the beginning of the year when he found out he had more than one daughter.

In it, his late wife held a daughter on either knee, one with emerald-green eyes and the other with sapphire blue ones and black veins around them. He stared at the portrait often, trying to forget any hate and regret he held within himself.

He hated his late wife.

Up until this year, he'd never loved her but he'd always respected her. She'd married him and been thrust into this royal life he wouldn't have wanted for anyone, and she'd never complained. It was only now that he knew that was because she'd wanted more of the royal life, more power.

He'd respected her as his wife.

And even more so when he'd learned that she'd risked a King's wrath in order to protect a daughter from his wrathful hand all those years ago. He'd been grateful to her.

Until the moment he found out the late Queen Rowena had been the one leading the rebellion. Until he found out she'd used her knowledge of his mind's inner workings to manipulate him into thinking Evony the rebel leader. Until she'd tried to kill both of his daughters.

He scoffed to himself. She'd even been the one to take Sparrow's father from him. The boy was a son to him, so it pained Edmund that she'd caused him such hurt.

Now he loathed her, but he'd always be thankful to her for two things. One, for birthing his daughters and two, for causing the rebellion that meant they needed to call on Evony.

He normally didn't look at the painting for her. He didn't want to ruin the painting in case his daughters one day wanted it, but normally, he kept a sheet over the top half of the painting to keep Rowena out of his sights.

But those two little girls.

He loved seeing them, seeing baby Evony. His little magician who'd been mercifully ripped from his life. As much as he hated to think on it, he'd still had the manipulations of his father in his head when she'd been born. He would've had her killed for being a magician.

It hadn't been until he'd begun raising Rosaelia that he'd understood love. And not until a few years ago did he understand it in its entirety.

Edmund sat back in his chair as he looked at the two little girls. They were beautiful, more like him than their mother.

Thankfully.

He sighed as his thoughts swirled to the one woman he'd want his children to take after.

He scoffed. How absolutely ridiculous. He'd kissed her once and was already subjecting her to bear his children. That thought would need to be kept locked away in his mind.

Though hidden away, his mind held onto the idea. The memory of kissing her making the desire stronger.

His grip on her face slowed her head from crashing as he threw her against the wall. She moaned into his mouth, not once hesitating to kiss him back. She allowed him to lead, and by the way she tugged on his arms and back, she wanted more.

He'd been reckless.

Allowing her to close that door was the single most difficult thing he'd ever done. And as King of the Northern Lands, he'd done some of the worst of the worst.

This was why he didn't allow himself to get near her. After being so close, how could he allow her to close the door on them?

Edmund didn't think as his fist slammed against her door.

And it didn't take but a few seconds for her astonished face to open it to him. "Your Highness?"

Nothing in this world would've been strong enough to keep him away as he stepped into her suite.

He couldn't tie their lives. In reality, when he was away from her, he knew it. It was the only time he was strong enough to stay away—when there was space between them. As much as it pained him, he needed to keep that space, make it stronger. He was a mask of a man, not worth her beauty. A shell with so much emotion left untouched. He had much care to take of himself before he would allow himself to drop it on a woman.

Another scoff rolled hard out of him. A woman? He didn't want a woman.

Atiana was his woman. At least, the only one he wanted even if their relationship never came to fruition.

He brought his tea to his lips and took a burning gulp, then dropped his head back and closed his eyes. He didn't care if Evony sent the whole of the Posse into his mind tonight. He couldn't stop from thinking of the way his beautiful tailor had moaned into his mouth.

"Edmund," she whisper-moaned as his mouth moved from her lips to taste her jaw, her ear, down her neck.

Her fingers desperately clung to him and the way her hips rocked against him, Edmund didn't fight it when his own hips rolled back then straight into her cunt. They had layers of clothing between them, but they both moaned at the touch.

He couldn't stop. Not until she had received her pleasure.

He licked up her neck until his tongue was in the warmth of her mouth once more, all the while rocking his hips into her so his cock fit perfectly against her cunt.

His hands, now gripped bruisingly at her thighs, held her in place as he thrust, his only goal to get her to that climax.

It wasn't long until her fingertips scraped at the back of his neck and she threw her head back. She was a mess of moans as he thrust his tongue into her mouth the way he desired to thrust his cock into her cunt.

When she finished coming, Edmund bit her bottom lip, then slowly pulled back enough to look her in the eyes. Her face was flushed, her mouth plump with evidence of his being there, and her eyes lust-drunk.

"Atiana," he growled, his hips rocking slowly now, teasing out any aftershocks as he tried to appease his own desire. It wouldn't happen though. He would not be coming. Not until she truly touched him, held him, tasted him.

CHAPTER 4
ATIANA

It was nearing winter. Nearing. Not quite that moment where snow littered the grounds—though not so much in their part of the North as further above—but no longer at a time where it was a nice cold. It was that time in late autumn when the winds could truly bite.

So it was Atiana's job to make sure all the clothes the group that had headed out to heal this plague would protect them when they came back. They'd already left, but not so far out yet. When they returned, Atiana would have these outfits ready. Five guards, Tristan, Norya, Gabriel, and Ashtyn. Seven men, two women.

Atiana began with the women's because ladies went first.

They would have warmed trousers to wear beneath their dresses—though only Ashtyn wore a dress on the day-to-day —and a jacket that would be worn over a vest for Norya or the dress for Ashtyn. The jacket was made of leather on the outside to keep them safe but of the softest fur on the inside to keep them warm. They might even berate Atiana that it is too warm after a while. But she did not care. Rather they be too warm than die of hypothermia.

All of the garbs—men's and women's—would be made of Atiana's best material, but the women's would get the prettiest of leathers. Norya's was a darker brown, like that of the deepest forests she'd likely survived in the Island. And Ashtyn's was a lighter brown, almost hazel, in order to compliment her eyes and hair, but also to compliment the fact that Ashtyn preferred to wear lighter-colored dresses. She was always in a cream or baby blue, light honey or the softest hues of pink and lavender.

Finished with their trousers and jackets, two for each, she readied socks for all nine of the travelers as the last thing they wanted was frostbite in their feet—though it wasn't yet quite that cold, Atiana knew the nights could become unbearable.

Only then did she move onto the seven men's garbs.

They would each be receiving the same set of trousers and jacket, though theirs would be more masculine and far larger to fit their frames. The men's jackets were closer to the same brown as Norya's, and because theirs were so much larger, there was more space for pockets. Atiana tried giving all nine of them ample space to store anything they might need, but she could not argue that the men's wardrobe left more room for it.

While preparing the final pieces of the jackets, Atiana hoped for their safety. She didn't know the guards all too well, and even Tristan she wasn't as familiar with, but the other three—Norya, Ashtyn, and Gabriel—Atiana had come to truly care for as friends. It felt surreal to have them in her life when for the longest time, her friends were only those who worked in the tailor's wing alongside her and the servants they spend their time with.

It was all thanks to Princess Rosaelia.

Both sisters had it in them. Rosaelia had brought her into

the mix, and Evony had brought Ashtyn. Now with the three of them, Norya, Etel, and Gemma, Atiana loved the girls' nights she spent with them. They would still be gathering in Norya and Ashtyn's absence but it would not be the same.

Atiana sighed and made herself forget the matter. They were doing something important and she was immensely proud of them.

It was with those thoughts that a smile tugged at Atiana's lips as she wondered if she were to sew a bright flower onto the men's jackets, whether they would still wear them. She could imagine Norya teasing them about it, and for that purpose specifically, she grabbed the jacket meant for Tristan and a lovely bright tulip for designs and sewed it to the front.

The winds blowing outside made Atiana go over her designs once more, making sure all of them were as warm as they could be. She was thinking about adding gloves to the mix as the fireplace in the tailor's suite—where she currently resided as there was more space than her suite—roared. Most of the others weren't around but she heard the talks of two of the younger tailors in the opposite end of the suite, in a smaller room as the tailor's suite was made up of one large room and a gathering of smaller spaces. Atiana was currently in the main one.

She didn't catch every word that was being muttered by those two but knew they were gossiping about Gabriel and Ashtyn, though she swore she heard whispers of the King's name as well.

With the mention and the winds hitting the windows, Atiana hoped Gabriel and Ashtyn, along with their entourage, were safely indoors for the night.

She smiled to herself as those two tailors came out of their ends and froze as if not expecting her to be sitting there. She hadn't been secretive of her work but Atiana tended to work quietly so she wasn't surprised they hadn't heard her, especially over the winds and their conversations.

She smiled at them, and they quickly returned it before running off.

Atiana then turned to begin internally measuring the amount of fabric that might be needed for gloves when a throat clearing brought her out of her thoughts, and when she looked up, her body reacted immediately to finding the King standing by the doors of the tailor's suite. "Your H—"

"Is Odolf here?"

She swallowed, taking him in completely. "No. It is his wife's birthday, and he gave the other tailors leave to take the day off."

"Why are you here?"

She shrugged. "I wish to complete these sets for Ashtyn and her group."

His gaze ate her up, then glanced around the room, landing on the pedestal before the mirrors used for measuring clients. "Right. Well, I will come back later then."

"I can help!" she squeaked, rising quickly to her feet. She offered him her assistance so many times before and he'd always refused. Would today be any different?

"I can wait for—"

"Please, Your Hi—"

"I told you not to call me that, Atiana."

She swallowed, remembering the exact distance his lips had been from hers when he'd made the demand. "Then allow me to help you."

He took a large breath in and seemed to never release it. Finally, he muttered, "I only need to be fitted for a new riding jacket."

"I just made Gabriel one not long ago. That would be absolutely no problem."

His eyes flashed at the mention of Gabriel's name, and he ground his jaw before moving for the pedestal. He removed the jacket he was currently wearing—one for around the palace and certainly not the outdoors—and stood ready for her.

They had his measurements, so Atiana wasn't sure why he'd needed to be fitted once more, but she would not argue this opportunity away.

The entire time she worked, he stood there stiffly. He was so handsome the way he looked off into space, so deep in thought, albeit he needed to relax.

"Your measurements may not be accurate if you do not relax."

"I am relaxed," he grit through his teeth.

Atiana bit the inside of her cheek to keep from laughing. What could possibly have him so stiff?

She looked up to the mirror to catch another glimpse of him, and couldn't help her blushing cheeks, her little smile she tried to keep contained. "What's got you so lost in thought, my King?"

"I shouldn't have done that," he whispered quickly.

"What?"

"Taken advantage of you."

Her brows furrowed as she stopped working and moved around to face him. "You didn't take advantage of me, Edmund." She let out a small gasp as his name left her lips.

His eyes widened hearing it, dilating to nearly black. She hadn't meant to say his name aloud again.

Atiana cleared her throat. "If I didn't want it, I would've pushed you away. King or not."

"Atiana—"

"Edmund. I wante—"

"Enough. You do not know what you're asking for, Atiana."

She scoffed. "What? Because I'm a tailor and not part of your inner circles, I must be an imbecile?"

"That is not what I said."

"But that is what you're thinking! That I must be so afraid, I would comply to make you happy. That I must be so stupid, I would think it easy to take the role as the King's woman? I'm sorry to break it to you, *my King*"—the words came out with venom this time rather than the love she'd been feeling before —"but you are neither as scary as you believe yourself to be nor as wise."

He stepped off the pedestal quickly, his hand wrapping around her throat and pushing her back. He never hurt her, though, as if he was very aware of the pressure he put on her. "Do not chastise me."

"No, you're right. What rights would I have? I am neither your woman nor a good enough tailor."

"Who the bloody hell believes you're not a good enough tailor?"

She almost scoffed that he chose to ignore the first part of her statement. "You do! Every time you insist on using Odolf, on waiting for Odolf rather than allowing me to help!" She was actually glad he'd chosen to focus on this topic. It'd been a pain she'd held for years, wanting nothing more than to create pieces for him but getting rejected every time. "It is not bad enough you do not approve, but the way you look at me when you refuse my services, as if I am a loathsome creature."

He scoffed. "Do not be so naive, Atiana!"

"Oh, so I *am* naive?"

He pushed her roughly against the wall, his free hand cradling the back of her head softly, completely juxtaposing the pure venom radiating off of him. "I go to Odolf because I cannot stand the thought of your hands on me!"

Her breath flew in but wouldn't release. Her hand was

itching to slap him when he said, "To know your hands are on me, and I cannot do a thing about it. I have control, Atiana, but not much. You saw it the other day. You had your hand delicately at my side, and I lost all sense. Can you imagine what I might do if they were running all over me? Measuring my inseams?"

"Edmund…"

"I go to Odolf to stay away from you, Atiana, because I'd be rather dangerous for you otherwise," he growled.

She was so stunned, it took her a moment to properly breathe again so she could form a cognitive sentence. Then she looked into his eyes with determination. "And who exactly made you my decision maker? Maybe I want whatever your dangers may be?"

I surely want it.

The thumb of the hand around her throat played with her bottom lip. "I want to get you pregnant, Atiana."

Her breath caught. "I wo—"

"I want to breed you," he breathed through clenched teeth. "To mark you." His hand at the back of her head fisted her hair. "To own you."

"And who's to say I wouldn't allow you to?" She tried her argument again.

His lips hovered over hers so closely they shared breath. His coming in hard as if he was fighting that control he'd spoken of. His hands tightened around her hair and neck, but he never hurt her. "You don't know what you're asking for."

"I think I do." *I know I do.*

"You would become Queen. The amount of gossip and hatred that would come your way. That can destroy a person not born into it."

"I can handle it."

"No. You cannot."

Now she was angry. "So naive, an imbecile, and weak? Any other compliments you'd like to give me?"

He gave a vile and cocky smirk, eyes the darkness that he always had for her, one that made her feel unwanted. "You come rather quickly. It took almost no work on my end."

Her breath caught. Why was that the most offensive of all? Was it her Northern upbringing? Either way, her hand flew through the little space between them and smacked him hard. "What is wrong with you?"

He finally released her and took a small step back, but not enough to give her any semblance of her own space. He scoffed, looking her up and down. "I thought you could take it, little tailor."

Her hand flew through the air again, but he caught it before it landed its strike this time. "Know your limits, Atiana," he growled.

"I hate you," she bit out, forcing the tears to wait until she was away from him.

She didn't mean it. They both knew it. But that didn't matter. She shoved his hand off of her and turned away before he could attempt another word. He could wait the rest of his life for Odolf for all she cared.

CHAPTER 5
EDMUND

He'd canceled every meeting for the day. He had half a mind to cancel them for the rest of the week, but as King, he could only take so much time off. He hadn't even wanted to cancel these, but there was no way he was going to be paying attention. Atiana took up every ounce of space within him.

"I hate you."

Had she meant it? The way she'd looked at him before he'd opened his stupid mouth proved she hadn't. It must've. He'd never seen her look at anyone like that before. Hell, he'd just barely kept himself from reaching for her with every glance she threw in the mirror. He'd been lucky to utter those words rather than give in to his selfish desires.

"You know everyone's scared you're going to lose it completely today," Evony's voice infiltrated his thoughts. "Apparently, King Edmund never cancels meetings."

Edmund turned only his head, hands still digging into the balcony he was leaning over. "Good. Let them fear me from time to time."

She stopped beside him, wearing a soft, knowing, close-lipped smile. "What happened with Atiana?"

His eyes narrowed. "You need to stay out of my thoughts."

She smirked. "I didn't need to get into your head to know what's going on in there."

He huffed, staring back out toward the forests beyond palace grounds. "Nothing's going on."

"Mm. And is that why you're so grumpy? Because nothing is happening again?"

"Evony," he chastised, and for once, he truly felt like her father. Though he was annoyed with her at the moment, he would cherish this moment later.

"One time! The one time I went into your head, you two were basically getting it on. I've only done it once."

He rolled his eyes. "And you'll keep it at that once."

"Yeah, yeah. So, was I right? Atiana?"

"Nothing will be happening with Atiana again."

"Why? Her thoughts are filled with you."

"Evony!"

"One time!"

"Evony," he chided.

"Okay, twice for her, but one of those times was because I thought she was checking Sparrow out and the baby hormones really didn't like that, but turned out she was just lost in thoughts about you. She has some dirty thoughts about you, you know. It was quite disturbing seeing my father in those positions, imagination or not."

The very last thing he needed was for his daughter to tell him about dirty thoughts.

Correction, the very last thing he needed was to know Atiana wanted him enough to get lost thinking of having him. In dirty ways especially.

His cock stirred, remembering the feel of her against his

body as he'd pushed her to orgasm, the way she'd lost herself in her moans. He wanted to do so again. Wanted, more than anything, to rip her clothes away and cherish every inch of her.

Which was exactly why he needed to stay away.

Evony's presence by his side was different from Rosaelia's. He hadn't raised Evony, so he didn't feel the need to hide certain parts of his life from her the way a father normally would. Both his daughters were grown now, neither innocent any longer, but Evony hadn't been innocent for a long, long time. There were certain things that seemed simpler for her to understand.

Or maybe it was because he didn't have to live up to the hero-dad image in her eyes. To her, they were only now becoming comfortable with the father-daughter dynamic.

"Even hidden as the Master, you'd always known the attention that brings. You cover yourself in garbs but you hold so much attention when you're called upon. There is so much gossip about you that you probably no longer hear it."

"That is true."

"Though you didn't grow up a Princess, the same attention followed you your entire life so when you came here, when you and Sparrow got together, the whispers didn't bother you. You were used to whispers being made about you."

She sighed as if she knew where he might be headed. "That is also true."

"Killian doesn't mind it because he had many whispers about him too. You cannot be a great warrior and not. He was in power once too. He knows what other's attention—in a negative sense—feels like, so he can easily brush it off."

Evony's fingers fidgeted on the stone railing as she glanced down at them, her soft voice telling him she knew where he was headed. "Yes."

"And Rosaelia isn't even Queen yet. Sparrow isn't King. Can

you imagine the harassment that would follow anyone with the King? The harassment that would come to a *common person* with the King?"

Her eyes closed and her shoulders fell as the words came out. "I'm sorry."

"For what?" he gruffed, back to staring out.

"I imagine the way you desire Atiana is how I do Sparrow. I cannot imagine staying away from him. It can only be the fiercest form of torture."

He scoffed. Did he feel for Atiana the way his daughters did their husbands? That would be absurd. He and Atiana had had all of a few real conversations in all the years of their acquaintance. That wasn't enough to fall in love with a person. "A jump, skip, and a hop, my daughter."

She quirked a brow.

"Assuming I feel for her even remotely close to what you do Sparrow."

She rolled her eyes. "Please. You're giving her up in order to protect her. You would only do that if your love for her outweighed your desire to be inside her."

His eyes rolled heavenward. "When will you learn to be appropriate around your father?"

She smirked. "Why would I ever do that? This is fun."

He shook his head but said nothing else.

"Anyway," she finalized, "I'm sorry. But..."

"But what?"

"Did she tell you she does not wish to be scrutinized?"

"She doesn't know what she wants."

Evony chortled. "Lords, men are stupid."

"Evony..." he chastised again, loving that he was beginning to feel so comfortable taking that tone with her.

"You know Atiana once told Etel there was an unrequited love that she would do anything for, take any bit of gossip for.

And come to find out that unrequited love is indeed very requited. It's been quite the year for the Posse and their relationships. Maybe it's finally your turn."

His heart raced. He could not—would not—think of what he'd just learned. It would do him no good. "You are rather annoying, Evony."

She giggled but said nothing more.

They were in such a comfortable silence, Edmund didn't want to break it, but finally he opened a different subject he'd been meaning to bring up to the Magician for a while. "I want to introduce you as a magician. We do not have to say the Master, but I want that introduction made as part of the campaign to allow magicians back." He cleared his throat. "And I'd like to introduce you as my daughter."

She was now staring off into the distance, her hand running gentle circles over her belly. "Sparrow won't like that. Especially right now."

"We can wait until you've given birth so your power is at its height. Until then, we can work with whoever Gabriel brings to the North."

She nodded. "I'd like to be part of the campaign that brings magicians back to the land my grandfather threw them out of. It would be rewarding."

Edmund's lips tipped up. "Ever the champion."

She winked in his direction. "It's in the Lenoir blood."

He scoffed. "You believe me a champion? Since when?"

"Since Sparrow won't shut up about it."

He laughed then.

As the silence carried, Edmund turned from the views and back to the exquisitely beautiful second daughter of his. "And what of the latter, Evony?" The very last thing she'd ever wanted was to be named a Princess, but would she concede?

Would she do this for the greater good? She shouldn't have to. He felt awful asking her to.

She swallowed, and he believed she wouldn't answer, when finally, she turned to meet his gaze and a small smile raised her lips. "I'd love nothing more than to be introduced as your daughter."

His heart thumped, and he almost lost his breath. There was no greater joy than the acceptance of a child so wronged throughout life.

I'll make sure you never regret it, he promised in his mind.

CHAPTER 6

EDMUND

It'd been nearly two weeks.

Nearly two weeks of staying away from her, of satisfying himself by watching her from a distance the way he had all these years.

Knowing what she tasted like, what she felt like clinging to him, what her breathy moans sounded like as she climaxed made it all the more difficult. Every time he felt himself moving for her rooms, Edmund had to convince himself to turn instead for the Posse's private training rooms. He hadn't been this sore since he was in his twenties but all the exercise was keeping him at bay, and that's what mattered.

His conversation with Evony still rang in his ears. The latter half made him happy, knowing she wanted to be named part of this family, knowing she was a Princess through and through by the simple way she was ready to take all the heat of the nation by being named a magician heir.

But he could not fight that first part of the conversation from coming back up, especially when the subject of his desires was standing just out of reach. Across the walkway beside the palace where he was now stopped with Ares and Wells, two of the five guards he'd sent with Ashtyn's traveling group, back without the others so they could give updates while Ashtyn continued on with her healing.

He'd only briefly met with them in the morning before allowing the lot to rest before getting a full report. But that brief meeting had been enough to learn of the Cousins.

"Their names are Astreya, Belinda, and Caetana," Ares opened.

Edmund smirked. "Cute."

"Yes, I can only imagine what the next would've been. Dirinda?" Wells joked.

They all smirked, leaning against the pillars as they discussed things.

Edmund didn't spend too much time with all of the guards, but the ones his boys thought trustworthy enough, Edmund had gotten comfortable around—and more importantly, they'd gotten comfortable around him—so they could all relax as they spoke. Which did complicate things because if they were all more serious at the moment, his rigid stance as he tried with all his might not to stare at Atiana wouldn't be as obvious, if at all.

Even so, neither man brought it up. Nor did they say anything about the way his gaze continued to slither over to the other end of the corridor where Atiana and Gemma were currently stopped discussing something.

It shouldn't have been shocking. As the most beautiful woman at the palace, the men probably only thought him appreciating her beauty the way every other man at this palace —lords, every man alive—did in passing.

"The Cousins," Edmund focused. "What do you two think? They're great magicians and can pass for Northerners but do you think they're trustworthy?"

Ares shrugged. "The whole lot of them that Gabriel introduced us to seemed trustworthy. I don't think they blame any of us for the laws here, and I think they're more glad about a possible rescind than angry about what had been in place."

Wells smirked. "Plus, there're other ways to put them in check. Gian has already started."

Edmund's gaze snapped from Atiana's beautiful smile to the man before him, narrowing. "I don't want any fuck buddy situation. We need them to remain here. No making it awkward and having to retreat."

Ares snickered. "Trust me, the way Gian hovers over Astreya and glares at everyone, they're more than fuck buddies."

Edmund narrowed his eyes. "You guys only found them a few days ago?"

Wells scoffed. "Love at first sight does happen, Ed. Look at Gabe. He's been bewitched with the healer since they met."

Edmund's gaze immediately jumped back across the corridor as his heart sped. He could believe in love at first sight, maybe, though he wasn't admitting to being in love with his tailor. He would argue lust at first sight, but he also understood what the men were saying—Gian wasn't hovering over his magician simply because he wanted to fuck her. He was hovering because he wanted her. All of her.

Edmund swallowed, turning back to the men hoping they weren't picking up just how much his attention drifted to that woman, especially with their current topic of conversation.

"Good."

Wells's smirk was still wide. "Though now that I know fuck buddies are apparently off the table, I need to get to know Caetana more."

Edmund narrowed his eyes. "You've already fucked her?"

He tsked. "Nah. Not yet."

"Wells," Edmund growled.

"Don't worry." He chuckled. "When this is all over, I'll figure it out with her. I won't fuck her until then, boss."

Ares smirked now. "You better lay claim soon then. Colt and Noah are with them right now. One of them can take Caetana."

Wells didn't take the bait. "I already told them she's mine."

"And not me!" Ares scolded.

"You're with me. I don't need to worry about you. Plus, you've got a thing for that tailor anyway, so I don't have to worry for shit."

Edmund stiffened, hating how so many other men wanted Atiana. "I didn't realize I was here to speak of your love lives."

Both men settled as they turned for Edmund when Wells said, "The others Gabe introduced us to were good people. I think they can come in handy in the future. Especially with all the magicians they have. If we need help in that regard, I think they'd be more than willing to help Gabe."

"Agreed," Ares said. "They didn't give off anything negative. Even Tristan and Gian were happy with them."

Being that Tristan and Gian were some of the best people readers, not to mention communicators, that gave Edmund some rest. "Anything else? With the Masters' council?"

They tsked as Ares said, "We could tell you what we learned of the healer, but the council didn't make any decisions. They learned of her past like they had with Sparrow, then made her heal some bad injuries. They wanted to keep going at it, but we all know our healer. She ate them for breakfast and spit them out. She wasn't having any of it."

Edmund chuckled. "Oh, I sure hope Gabriel can control her."

They smirked as Wells said, "I think so."

"Speaking of controlling women." Ares's hand glided down

his chest and stopped at the edge of his trousers. "I need to go find Liliana. I think she'd like to know I'm home for the night."

"Liliana?" Edmund's gaze snapped from where Atiana and Gemma were still laughing.

"His tailor," Wells explained.

His tailor? Liliana?

Edmund sighed. "Right. Well, go then. I don't need much else from you boys. Rest up, enjoy yourself. You're back on the road in the morning."

They both gave a single nod and turned away together, Wells heading for the training barracks with the other guards and Ares turning toward the palace to hunt down his woman.

Edmund remained standing there.

Liliana. He was going to find Liliana.

Atiana was still his.

As she and Gemma turned away, heading into the palace as well, Edmund's heart beat faster. No. Atiana wasn't his. She couldn't be.

But he also didn't know if he was strong enough to see her with anyone else.

CHAPTER 7
ATIANA

tiana decided while Gabriel wasn't around to give her those riding lessons, she would take up Gemma's offer to go with her to the Remedies Expert and learn some concoctions. They'd been discussing a set of matching outfits for her and Evony's babies—whether same sex or not—in the corridor as Atiana tried not noticing Edmund out of the corner of her eye, tried not fixating on the way his stare burned into her profile.

So, yes, going to the Remedies Expert sounded exceptionally nice.

Plus, it added toward the goal for the new her—the Atiana who wasn't afraid and was open to new experiences. And the top of way she wished to create that woman was by learning more. She'd started the task by asking Norya for help with weapons like she helped Etel, then moved on to horses, but while Norya and Gabriel were away, Atiana had accepted the delay and continued on with life. But now, she was given an opportunity to learn more once again, so she would be joining Gemma in the remedies room. There was so much to learn, and these people she was fast becoming friends with were some of the best teachers. She also couldn't wait because all of the women had asked for some more help on intricate designs from her, so she would also be able to teach them in return.

When they got to the room, a guard was rushing out with a mini purple vial that was likely for pain or headaches or the sort. Etel was standing by the large table in the middle while her husband sat on a stool behind her and massaged her sides. The only other person was Nona Eleni, who sat quietly by the slightly open window taking in the cold air outside as she picked herbs for their stores. Though the woman was Northern by blood, she'd spent decades in the Island, so Atiana could imagine she missed the cool weather. She knew from Princess Rosaelia's visits that Killian missed it.

"I got a friend to join!" Gemma exclaimed as she stopped on the other side of the large table and reached for a cloth to wrap around her face.

"How amazing!" Etel remarked, continuing to fill the final three vials with a light pink liquid.

Atiana took in Gemma's look then glanced around. "Do we need to wrap our faces?"

"Oh no." Etel smiled. "Because of the baby, a lot of smells don't agree with Gem so she covers up so she doesn't smell them. As long as the smells don't end up bothering you, you should be fine."

"Lovely."

Miels watched her from over his wife's shoulder, and for some reason Atiana stood taller. It felt like she was being tested on whether or not she'd be good enough for the King, even though said King had already told her he didn't intend on making her his. Even still, Atiana wanted to leave Miels, one of the King's most important men, with a good impression.

"Was there something in particular you wanted to learn?"

Etel asked as she finished off her vials and placed the cauldron aside for washing.

"No." Atiana pinked. "Gemma just mentioned she was headed here, and I thought it could be fun."

Miels scoffed. "With the amount she complains, I'm surprised you got that impression."

A wooden spoon flew at the man's head but he caught it without a glance, then winked in Gemma's direction as she harrumphed. "I do not complain that much. And certainly not when it's only me and your wife. You're simply a bad instructor."

He chortled. "I'm a fabulous instructor."

Etel's lips tipped up in what looked like a fight to keep her smile in.

Gemma didn't let it go unnoticed. "You see! Even your wife thinks you're bad!"

Miels instantly turned his wife around, grabbing her by the face and forcing her to look at him. What he saw there must've confirmed Gemma's statement because he scoffed, his fingers digging into her scalp. "You think I'm a poor instructor?"

Atiana couldn't see her face, but she imagined a cheeky smile on the expert's face. "You're not *the* best."

Miels's eyes narrowed as he glanced at Atiana over his wife's head. "Would you allow me to teach you?"

Atiana felt everyone's—but Etel who was held in place by her husband—eyes on her almost like this was a challenge. Her own lips tipped up. Even if it was a challenge, it sounded like a fun one. "Of course."

Miels gave his wife a satisfied look. "Now you must watch me with the most beautiful woman at the palace. You see your mistakes?"

Atiana's cheeks pinked. She knew people referred to her as such, but she didn't like when it was used for matters. She never wanted her looks to be the reason she got anywhere in life or the reason behind a couple breaking up.

But the expert only laughed. "Unless she throws you out for being an awful instructor."

Miels growled, then leaned in for a very inappropriate kiss. When he finally pulled away, he smirked at his woman. "We'll see how awful an instructor I am when I get you to our suite later."

Etel turned pink. Even with her back to Atiana, that much was obvious. Every inch of her exposed skin turned pink. "Are you going to make me beg?"

Etel asked it in such a soft voice, Atiana only heard it because of years of listening to people whisper. It was a skill she hadn't realized she had until a few years ago when she'd been able to hear a lot of secrets that were definitely meant to remain between two people. And Etel had certainly whispered it. She was more inbred with Northern customs than Atiana herself.

Miels's light response even had Atiana's body tingling. "You'll wish we'd end at begging. You're going to be desperate for me, my creature. You're going to completely lose your mind."

Again, the Remedies Expert grew pink.

Gemma's laugh from beside her brought Atiana out of staring at the two. "Don't worry about those two. They always end up whispering what I can only assume are dirty things by the way Etel turns pink at least three times in a given day. You'll get used to it."

Atiana smiled. She certainly hoped she got used to it. Not because her Northern upbringing made her uncomfortable with the displays but because she figured getting used to it meant these people would've grown as close friends to her. She suspected the fact that they felt comfortable to do this in front of her to begin with meant she was at least halfway there.

"Yes, I'm still waiting for the day they forget there are others around and he lifts her skirts." The voice came from the edge of the room where the always quiet Nona Eleni worked. She didn't react as all eyes snapped to her, continuing her work as if she hadn't just spoken, and Atiana loved her more for it, to have that much confidence. It must've come from all her years in the Island.

"Don't worry, Nona." Miels grinned as his hands traveled down Etel's body and cupped her butt. "I know you've become accustomed to a certain way in the Island. I'll give you a show one day."

Atiana's blush was as deep as Etel's now as the others laughed.

"Okay, enough!" Etel pushed her husband away. "Go show us your great instructing."

Miels smirked, coming for Atiana's side. "I would wager if I win, then we must start creating our heir, but I already fuck you all the time, and I've already changed your concoctions to placebos so they don't disrupt your ability."

Etel's head snapped to him, eyes narrowing, and Atiana wasn't sure if the man was kidding. Whether he was or not though, Etel didn't seem to mind.

Atiana's cheeks pinked again. It must've been baby-wanting season for men. James and Sparrow had already gotten their wives pregnant. Miels had been speaking of it for months now. And Edmund had...

I want to breed you.

She desperately wanted to allow him to.

MIELS ENDED up being a far better instructor than she'd been preparing herself for, and Atiana had the best afternoon in a long time with the four of them. But when they'd gone their separate ways after hours together, Atiana decided she'd take dinner with the servants as that was how she had normally took her meals. Before this growing friendship with the Posse that she still couldn't believe was happening, Atiana's time was either spent alone or with servants. They were friends. None she'd consider as close as she felt herself growing with the women of the Posse but friends still.

She was walking from the kitchens with Ila, Dorothy, and Quintina toward the servants' rooms at the bottom of the palace before she and Dorothy needed to move for the tailor's wing.

Atiana spent much of the walk silently listening as was her usual forte.

"Lords, the way Miels has fallen besotted over Etel, I would wonder if she were a sorcerer with access to love potions if I hadn't seen her work with my own eyes," Quintina shrieked. "That man loves her so earnestly."

Atiana's lips tipped up as the others shrieked, speaking of their own encounters witnessing the Remedies Expert and Posse spy. Atiana herself felt giddy thinking of it. Those two were completely gone for one another. Miels especially with the way he could have an entire conversation with someone while keeping his eyes glued to his wife.

"Do you think that's how the Posse's relationships are?" Ila asked. "Real? They look real from the outside, like the Assassin is obsessed with his wife, and the barbarian with the Princess, but how real are they truly? The spies are basically heirs with the Assassin. Don't you think they're faking it?"

"I have that same theory, I," Dorothy smirked. "Everyone knows royals marry for advantage. I have a bet they're marrying strategically and making it look like love to convince us otherwise."

Atiana snorted at the ridiculousness. She's been around every single one of those couples and they were all gone for one another. "And what reason would any of the partners give? None of them are higher ranking."

Well, except Evony as an heir and a Master herself. But they didn't know that.

Dorothy quirked her brow. "I suspect the Assassin chose his wife because of her blood connection to the crown. The Princess's cousin? That means no matter the situation, the crown would move to them if anything happened to the King and Princess."

Atiana didn't allow herself to roll her eyes. That theory was a popular one that sprung up when their betrothal was announced and hasn't died down since.

"As for the Princess," she continued. "We do not know who this Killian truly is. He could be royalty there for all we know. I reckon he is. Look at the scars on his face, the ones on his body when he removes his shirt to train..." She shook her head with a bit of fear in her eyes. "I reckon he's proved himself in the Island and they made a strategic marriage to either open back with the Island or for some other measure."

That one, though false, made sense given no one knew who Killian was. And again, it was another popular theory. Along with the fear for Killian.

But he wasn't a scary man.

Sure, he was quiet and moved with a dark look about him but that was simply because of the savage life he'd lived before where he had to constantly be ready for a fight to the death. The way he was around Rosaelia, softly watching her and smiling at her and touching her, he was the epitome of *in love*.

"Those are the popular theories, sure, but what of the others then?" Atiana argued.

"Norya must be a high-ranking member too," Ila added. "Tristan took her in for that."

Quintina snorted. "And I am not convinced Etel isn't a sorcerer. A love potion to move herself up the ranks from a lowly servant to a role made specifically for her to then within the Posse? Please. She definitely maneuvered her way in."

"You know," Ila continued, "she could be working her love potions within all the spouses of the Posse. Think of it. Before any of them came along, the Posse was Northern and kept their sexual appetites hidden as we all do. Even the spies who whored around. But then they come around and we cannot turn a corner without catching Tristan and Norya, and sometimes even the others!"

Dorothy snapped her fingers with a gasp. "That couldn't have been her plan all along. Bring along a marriage for the Assassin so it would be inconspicuous when she moved in on one of the members. And genius too, to not get the next highest ranking member."

"It does make you wonder who she is working with to get with the King, does it not?" Quintina shook her head. "How deliciously conniving. And a brilliant way for the lot of them to work their way up in power. I imagine..."

Atiana swallowed, not listening any longer. Was this how people would speak of her if they found out about that kiss she'd shared with the King? What if they found out how much more she wanted from him, and he from her? If they found out he wanted to breed her—a fact she still felt herself flushing with excitement over—how would they treat her then? Would they be friends still or would they speak of her like this when she wasn't around?

She internally scoffed. Of course they would speak of her when she wasn't around. The real question was—would she care?

Atiana glanced over to the women still speaking ill of the Posse relationships. They were her friends, no doubt of it, but after spending time with the Posse women, could she truly call them friends? After what she'd experienced with Rosaelia and Gemma and Ashtyn and the whole lot of them, this didn't feel like enough. It was very surface-level.

Glancing back out at the corridor they walked, Atiana knew what she'd always known. Of course she'd risk it. It would hurt, surely, to have women she thought of as friends speaking of her such, but with all the happiness she had to gain, Atiana couldn't find it in herself to care.

"At!" Dorothy demanded, catching Atiana out of her thoughts. "There you are! What were you thinking of so fixedly."

Atiana shook her head. "Nothing."

The girl smirked but didn't push her. "Tell us, At."

"What?"

"You spend more time with the Posse than anyone we know. It's you or Odolf they go to for tailoring. What of the relationships? Fake, no?"

Atiana met each one's gaze and noticed how desperately they wanted gossip, and she could not blame them. They were excited by the secrecy that came with being in the Posse, given they had an entire nation to run. "I've never experienced love like it. They are each made for one another."

All three women smiled, but it was clear that wasn't the response they'd hoped for. Still, Ila grinned. "Well, oo la la, let us all find loves like that."

Atiana smiled but it did not meet her eyes. She'd already found a love like that, and he refused her.

Her heart ached at the reminder she pushed aside as she continued listening to the women's relationship gossip once more, this time about other servants. And somehow, though they did speak of people who were merely sleeping together, they did not find it unreasonable as they had with the Posse that man and woman could be in love.

"That way Juac touches Ini," Ila sighed. "He is obsessed with her, and I…"

GABRIEL WASN'T AROUND but Atiana had had a single lesson with him before he'd left for his journey with his wife. That lesson, though definitely not much, would have to be enough because Atiana was antsy with the need to do something active.

She'd come out just before daybreak, unable to sleep and unwilling to toss around any longer, and hadn't realized her feet had taken her to Absko until she was stopped before him.

The boy was standing as if waiting for her, and he neighed like he was excited she was the one to show up.

Atiana smiled at the animal as she brushed her hand down his nose. "Hi, Absko. I've missed you too."

He nodded at her attention, and Atiana smiled as she handed him the apple she'd picked up from a pack at the other end of the stables. "Here, boy. You enjoy this while I try to figure out how to saddle you."

It took a bit of time and even then, Atiana was almost certain she'd missed a step or three, but it would need to be good enough. They would be going slow anyway.

She moved him by the reins until they were out of the

stables, then stepped on a stool to mount him rather than attempting to do so the way Gabriel had shown her. She thankfully had her trousers and jacket on rather than a dress as if she'd subconsciously known she would end up here, but still, she did not wish to fall while trying to mount without the stool.

Absko waited patiently, almost as if he was chuckling at her attempts.

Once atop, Atiana leaned down, petting him. "Good job, Absko. Thank you for being so patient with me. Now, please be gentle and slow too."

He listened.

They slowly left the stables, and Absko walked around the greens, moving as if he'd make a large circle.

After the first few minutes, Atiana relaxed enough to take in a large breath and speak to her companion. "You know, Absko, I'm in love with your owner." As he shook his head, she giggled. "Yes, yes, I know. Ashtyn has informed me of how cliché that is. But I cannot help it. He is such a good man. An arrogant, obnoxious man who thinks he knows everything, but a good man still.

"I understand why he's doing it, you know. He kissed me, then came to see me only a few days later to tell me it was a mistake. Can you believe that? He told me, in one fell swoop, that he both wanted to get me pregnant and that what we'd done was a mistake. He is such an ass, Absko." He moved his head as if agreeing. "But I understand better now. I always have, don't get me wrong. I've listened to the help around the palace, whether servants or other tailors or the medics, I've heard all of them gossip, and especially of those within the Posse. And normally, it's not very nice. I know Edmund is doing this to protect me. But, Absko, I don't want it. I don't care what they say of me. I want him."

Absko moved his head again, neighing as if speaking.

And though she didn't understand him, Atiana felt that she did. "He is quite a bit older, yes, and you're right, that will come with its own complications. I mean, I am only eight years older than his daughters, while he is sixteen years older than me. But... I don't know, I don't think his daughters would mind." She sighed. "I should figure that out, though, shouldn't I? I do not wish to ruin my relationship with them, especially not Rosaelia. I have come to love her dearly.

"But let us say all is well with them. Do you not think then that there is nothing truly standing in our way?" With another round of noise from the horse, Atiana laughed. "Yes, you're right. Edmund will stand in our way. Back to his being an ass, how could I forget?"

Starting another lap around the greens, Absko huffed around as if rehashing his own story. This time, Atiana didn't fully understand the horse, but she felt that she got the gist of what was being relayed.

"You are already loyal to him, are you, boy?" Atiana brushed his mane as he nodded his agreement. "I am glad." After giving him a soft kiss, she sat back up. "And would you be just as loyal if the weight up here got heavier? I've long wanted to ride with him."

Absko jostled with excitement.

Atiana laughed, throwing her head back. "Truly? That excites you?"

He jostled some more as if dancing with each step.

Still, she somehow knew what he was saying. "Oh, you dirty, dirty horse. Of course, you're a man. How could I be shocked? But I said we would ride together. I said nothing about him touching me in any indecent way."

The horses snickered, disgruntled now, and Atiana could not help the continued giggles.

"You filthy thing," she teased.

As Atiana fully smiled for the first time in days, she sat more confidently on her horse, slowly leading Absko around the greens—though she was sure he was doing more the leading and making sure she wouldn't freak out. She favored him even more for it.

As she turned from the rising sun before daybreak, Atiana subconsciously pulled on the reins to stop Absko in his trek.

Standing at the other end of the greens, leaning against the stables with his hands folded before his chest, was the man of all her desires. Watching her. And in his eyes, she saw a glimmer of... joy?

Unfathomable. He seemed to live to push her away. Why would he be happy to see her, least of all after she'd stolen his horse. The one he liked to ride in the mornings.

And still, Atiana sat tall. She didn't care that she'd stolen the King's horse. Matter-of-fact, she narrowed her eyes in his direction as if daring him to say something to her.

His lips twitched up, and his eyes twinkled, but he did not move.

Atiana's heart sped up. He looked so glorious.

And was he... enjoying this?

Her brows furrowed now, not to push at him any longer but because she wasn't sure what was going on with him. He was the one to push her away, yet out here with no one to witness them, he looked content to watch her ride his horse.

Atiana didn't allow herself to overthink it and instead turned Absko to continue walking the greens but never allowing him to get too close to the King.

Eventually he'd leave. Even if that eventually meant she'd have to endure an hour of his beautiful dark eyes following her.

CHAPTER 8
EDMUND

He'd have liked to stick around and watch her ride his horse all day and night, but two things stopped him. First, he had a meeting with his magicians committee group to introduce them to his daughter. And second, he couldn't have others coming out and finding him watching her with all the feeling she was allowing out. That was the whole reason he couldn't allow them to be together—to keep gossip away. He definitely wouldn't add to it by standing around ogling his beauty.

It took everything in him to finally turn away as the day officially began. With his back to her, Edmund felt her eyes piercing into his back, and couldn't help from imagining her nails doing the same. Fuck, he wanted to make her come again. This time with far fewer clothes on.

The memory of her moans and the feel of her cunt riding his trouser-clad cock accompanied Edmund until he made it to his meeting room where the magicians council he'd set up were already waiting for him. Edmund adjusted his length to make sure the dent wasn't obvious, then nonchalantly made his way in. As always, he remained silent as he made his way to the head of the table. Only a few minutes later, Sparrow and Evony walked in.

She had her hand clasped around his arm like she always did and her other hand resting on her rounded belly. She was forced to wear dresses now in order to comfortably fit even though she preferred her trousers and vests, and she wasn't always happy about it. The long-sleeved piece looked beautiful on her, soft and inviting for any expecting mother. Being that she was nearly six months along now, it wouldn't be long until Edmund became a grandfather.

He internally scoffed. He would become a grandfather soon, yet he spent his nights thinking of getting Atiana *pregnant*.

His council quieted with their appearance given they were not made aware of the day's plan, and tracked the two carefully as Sparrow closed the doors behind them. He made his way to the chair at Edmund's side, which had specifically been left open, and took it, dropping his wife into his lap.

It was clear the show of intimacy was bewildering to the rest of the council with their wide eyes and high brows. It often made Edmund remember that he'd felt the same way at the beginning of the year the first time he'd walked into the dining hall to find his new daughter in the lap of the man he'd raised as a son. It was none of their faults. Their Northern blood made it so.

But even now with that round belly, Evony preferred her husband's lap.

And especially now with that round belly, Sparrow preferred it. As if he could keep her safer somehow if she were in his lap.

Edmund's chest snagged with a beat of jealousy. He could picture himself holding a certain woman in his lap as well, could easily picture her with a rounded belly as she sheltered herself in his arms. He wanted it so deeply, it almost took his breath away.

He cleared his throat, fighting the ache building in his chest, and turned to the others who sat expectantly. "There are a few things that will become public knowledge at the end of Evony's pregnancy, and I wanted to share them with you first. Then we can all make a plan on how to best proceed."

They all sat up, still eyeing the Master Assassin like they were afraid of what this could mean, especially if it was in regard to his wife whom he'd made a point to demonstrate meant the world to him.

"We started this council as a way to figure out how to once again reopen the allowance of magicians into our lands. That meant we needed to figure things out, and you lot have been an important part of that," Edmund credited his team. "And with Gabriel out with Ashtyn, we now have a whole group of magicians in the southern parts of the Southern Lands that could help us if we need it, but we also have the three magicians they picked out to help them."

"I knew they would be looking. They found three they can trust?" Asha asked.

"They did. A set of cousins. From what we've been told, they likely have Northern blood because they could easily pass as one of us."

Aliyev nodded. "That will certainly help. If the public sees that magicians are not only Southerners by blood but that anyone could've become one. It will be nice especially for those families who somehow had a magician baby and had to drop their lives here and move down to the South."

Edmund nodded. "Yes, hearing they were Northern by blood was definitely a plus I hadn't been expecting. But the plan with them was always to get them here to help with the plague first—which would then demonstrate to Northerners that magicians won't be out to get them or hurt them. They are aware that we will want them to represent the coming of magicians once again."

All four of his members nodded, then Yarro cleared his throat. "And what does this have to do with the Master's wife?"

Edmund sat straighter and met his daughter's eyes. They were such a beautiful sparkling blue, and they looked back at him with trust. His heart ached all over again, this time for receiving the one thing from his daughter he thought he'd completely ruined.

Then he turned back to the others. "When Evony came to the North, we introduced her as a cousin from Rowena's side. Did you believe that?"

They all looked uncomfortable, but it was Asha who finally answered, "I found it off given I'd heard so much that Princess Rosaelia looked like your side, not her mother's, but I didn't think it outrageously inconceivable. Plus, I figured if she was from your side, she surely would've said it as that was far more a guarantee to the line than being from Rowena's."

"I had similar thoughts," Aliyev stated.

"I figured it was a lie," Vardan announced. "I didn't understand why she might like to go along with it given the connection to you would be stronger, but I'd also heard of the uncanny resemblance of your mother to the Princess. I didn't think it possible she was anything but a bastard daughter."

Sparrow's arms visibly tightened around his wife, but neither Master commented.

"I... was able to convince myself it was true and a lie. I bounced around a lot and never really settled," Yarro finalized.

Edmund swallowed as he was finally going to voice something he'd wanted to for months to those outside the Posse.

"You were right. Rosaelia does look like my mother, and that was simply something I had to hope didn't catch on with most of the population. But Evony is my daughter."

All four nodded, patiently waiting.

"Not only my daughter but a legitimate daughter."

Eyes widened as Asha remarked, "But I swear history remembers Queen Rowena only pregnant once."

Edmund nodded. "She was. With twins."

Everyone's gaze shot to his second heir, then back to him.

"She had Evony a few minutes after Rosaelia with only her nursemaid in the room to help her. When Evony was born, they decided to hide her from me."

Those shocked eyes turned to outrage, and Vardan demanded, "Who the bloody hell did she believe herself to be to keep a father from his daughter?"

Given Vardan had four daughters, Edmund imagined the thought of any of his daughters being hidden from him pained him more than anything else in the world.

"I'm glad they did."

Now the outrage was aimed at him.

"Why?" Yarro asked, more inquisitive than angry.

Asha and Vardan allowed enough anger to make up for it though.

"She was born with black veins around her eyes. An unmistakable—"

"Magician," Asha gasped as everyone turned for Evony.

Edmund swallowed, but everyone was too busy watching his daughter to pay him any mind. "I wasn't the same man back then as I am now. I would've... I would've had her killed. My late wife was deplorable in many ways, but for keeping my second heir from me, I will always be thankful."

"The Northern royal bloodline has a magician?" Aliyev voiced.

"A very powerful one," Edmund answered. They wouldn't mention her Masterhood. At least, not yet, but he could remark on her power.

"Remarkable," Aliyev eyed her with awe.

"So along with the Cousins, we will have my wife," Sparrow finally commented. "She will be presented as an heir, a magician heir."

Asha softly cleared her throat. "May I ask why she hasn't already?"

Evony gave a soft smile. "I didn't want it. Even now, knowing everyone will refer to me as Princess makes me sick. I do not want it. But if it will help with opening passage for magicians, it will not be a large price to pay."

Vardan snickered. "Especially with the Assassin as your husband. No one will attempt to upset you."

"Lucky me." Evony's lips widened into the most proud grin possible, and again, Edmund found himself jealous. He wanted a certain woman grinning proudly for him.

"Well." Yarro sat back. "This will certainly make planning more interesting."

ALONE WITH ONLY HIS THOUGHTS, Edmund had forced himself to the top room of the palace where Sparrow normally liked to read his missives. Sitting in the privacy of the office in his suite was dangerous. With no one else around, it was too easy to remember breathy moans and a delectable body pressed against his and far too tempting to open his trousers and take his cock in hand.

At least here, it was far more likely for someone to walk in.

Safe.

Well, safe enough.

In his hand, Edmund had the missive from the South regarding Ashtyn. She'd gone down to be tested to find out whether she was a Master Healer. Though he knew a lot of things, how Masters were determined was still a mystery to Edmund, and even to Sparrow who made it his mission to know everything about everyone. All the Assassin had been able to pick up was those sitting on the council had gone through lifelong trainings of all sorts before they were given their positions. They were masters in their own right, though not naturally as Masters were. Masters of Masters.

In the letter, they wrote to inform Edmund of how unprofessional they found Ashtyn to be and how they thought it rude that she yelled at them and stormed away, refusing to stay for any more tests. Edmund chuckled to himself the entire time he read it because he would've expected nothing less of the girl. The council had been lucky she'd agreed to go at all. They'd have to make do with what they had learned, going into their studies to make sure all the pieces fit. The letter ended, informing him they were lucky to gather enough of that information, but that it would take a few extra days for them to make their conclusions.

Either way didn't matter to Edmund. If she was a Master, it was merely to explain her abilities. It would also put all eyes on Edmund because then he'd have two—known—Masters within his circles. Lords, if Evony ever came out, the brutality of everyone's comments would come in thick—the conniving King of the Northern Lands, strategically and skillfully not only got three Masters—powerful ones at that—but got them to be loyal as well.

Another reason to keep Atiana out of the heat. As his wife, she would bear the brunt of the criticism.

But even if Ashtyn wasn't determined a Master, it would

not change her abilities. She would still be able to do everything she could, and Edmund always appreciated her efforts, even when he wasn't always the best at showing it.

Placing the Southern missive aside given there was no need for a response, Edmund picked up another very important piece of paper. This one had a simple crest stamped onto the top, one that was clumsily made. Given the people were still trying to make their way, that didn't surprise him. He was glad for the No Known Housing group who had taken up residence in the estate that had once been Killian's before his scars. And glad even more so that his own daughter had made an acquaintance who was a skilled sorcerer. A young one who was willing to correspond with them. These were the first steps to a long journey. One that would hopefully end up with opening all borders.

But it would be a long journey.

One Rosaelia might have to be ruling for.

One he might not live long enough to see. That's how different Islanders were from Northerners and Southerners.

This letter was from the Housing group telling him of the types of things they would be able to begin producing in order to trade with the North. That way they wouldn't become a charity case, the North wouldn't hold anything over them by being the saviors, and everyone within the Housing could hone in on skills.

Listed were bullet points of different products and approximately how much they thought they could complete per fortnight when Edmund would send a boat to trade with them. They finished it with their own question.

Edmund placed the paper down and picked up a clean one and his quill, preparing to write out everything they would be willing to trade and for what. Being an entire nation, Edmund had more room for negotiation, but he was a fair man. He would give them a great deal. It was both because a few women in his life had turned him particularly mushy but also because he saw the advantage to treating them well. This was the very beginning of their partnership. They'd have a long way to go, and the Housing unit could come in very handy in the future.

CHAPTER 9
ATIANA

Another early morning was spent riding Absko around the greens. They'd gone slow like before, and Atiana didn't see herself getting any more adventurous until Gabriel was back around to help her, but she'd had a wonderful time.

Up until she'd noticed Edmund watching her from a distance once more.

She hadn't wanted to go to him, at least that's what she told herself, but Absko had other plans. The horse moved immediately for his owner, disregarding any of Atiana's attempts to pull on his reins to stop him. Given she'd hardly had any lessons, Atiana figured she was probably doing it wrong to begin.

Stopped before the King, Atiana breathed in and out slowly, controlled, before slowly sliding her leg around and balancing on the stirrup. She'd gotten off using the stool before, so she worried about the fall.

Until two large, strong, warm hands clasped around her waist, and she froze. Clearing her throat, Atiana didn't move from where she was balancing leaning on the horse as words left her. "I thought touching broke your control."

"I won't let you fall, Atiana." He said the words in a clipped tone, so maybe he was struggling to rein in control. She hoped so for all the heartache he was putting her through.

Either way, she didn't have time to think on whether to allow his help or not because his hands tightened on her waist before bringing her down. Standing with her back to his front, Atiana was afraid to turn around, basking in the feel of his breath on her hair.

"You smell mouthwatering, Atiana."

"Stop saying my name."

"Why?" he whispered.

She swallowed, then forced herself to turn around, not shocked to find hardly any space between them. She'd felt his heat on her back. "I want you, Edmund. I know you believe I cannot handle the gossip, but I don't care about it. I am friends with your group already. Already, I have to defend them. It will not affect me as direly as you're imagining."

He watched her intently, and Atiana liked to imagine he was picturing her with his daughters. Making her his would only be possible if she had a positive relationship with not only his daughters but the entire Posse. How exciting could it possibly be that she was already friends with them? Knowing she would defend them must've been his ultimate deciding factor because he gently moved his hand to her face.

"You are beautiful, and that is why everyone wants you, Atiana." He spoke so plainly. "You think anyone would be shocked to find that you're in my bed? Not a single person will. The second it's heard of, everyone will 'know' you've been warming my bed for seven years, and that's why I haven't stepped out with anyone. They'll think your station came from the things you allow me to do to you and not your talents."

"That is my brunt to bear."

He stroked a soft finger down her face, moving a piece of hair behind her ear. "You want to be known as my whore?"

Her eyes widened. "Excuse me?"

"That's what you'll be seen as. My whore. And because of your beauty, everyone will believe I have chosen you because every man wants you."

"Your worry about it already makes me know otherwise." Though her chest hurt at thinking anyone would think of her as a whore, as the woman who was merely there to warm his bed and spread her legs.

"But it's true, Atiana." His finger grazing her cheek made it take far longer for her to hear his words than it should've. "You caught my eye because of your beauty. The same way you caught everyone's eye. I wanted you in my bed because I knew your beautiful face would lead to a sinful body."

"I want you to find me beautiful, Edmund. I want you to yearn for my body. I certainly do yours." She didn't know where her confidence was coming from considering she'd thought he hated her for years, but knowing he wanted her so much he was willing heartache to protect her made her stand tall with the words.

"What if I said you will be nothing more than a body to me? Would you take the rumors then? I can give you the space in the King's wing if you'd like, but what if I said you were to become my whore. I already have legitimate heirs. I can still breed my whore."

She swallowed her bile. "You wouldn't."

Absko moved behind her like he felt her discomfort and wanted to help her. He couldn't, but Atiana loved him more for it.

"I would, Atiana. Tell me you'll spread your legs for me, and I will."

A long beat of silence passed between them in which Atiana tried to find the truth in his eyes. He was so good at masking his emotions, and though she felt herself in love with him, she didn't know him, not really. She certainly didn't know him well enough to be able to tell his lies from his truths. As king, his entire life has been based on showing everyone outside the Posse that reading him was impossible.

Finally, she realized they were alone and he did not need to hide anything. He'd had two weeks since their argument in the tailor's wing to come up with how he could still fuck her and not truly have her.

But she would be no one's whore.

"I really do, Edmund," she finally whispered, shaking her head, tears stinging the backs of her eyes because she wouldn't allow them out. "I hate you."

"ATIANA, will you tell me what's wrong?" Rosaelia's voice broke her out of her thoughts.

"What?" she whispered.

"You're upset," the Princess said, standing still as Atiana placed a pin into the extra fabric at her side. "Please allow me to help you."

Atiana glanced up from where she stood behind the Princess on the mini pedestal, finding her beautiful green eyes in the mirror. "Nothing is wrong."

Rosaelia's shoulders dropped as she turned to face her. "Atiana, please. We are friends, aren't we? I want to be friends with you more than anyone else at this palace. Will you not trust me?"

"Why?"

"Why trust me?"

"No. Why do you wish to be my friend?"

Rosaelia's lips lifted softly. "I cannot explain it. I feel as if we are kindred spirits. We're both Northern in upbringing, both blush at certain talk, both of us are quiet listeners. I'd like to say we're both good at advice, but you certainly win there. I feel a connection to you. I hate that it took years of you working here for me to come up with the courage to be closer to you, but I'm an adult now—especially now—and I know we can have much in common."

Atiana was shocked to hear the words. They didn't only sound sincere, but she was shocked by how right they they were. She felt the same way.

"Why are you looking at me like that?" Rosaelia was holding both of her hands, looking at her with wide eyes and a hopeful, wide smile.

"I just... I didn't realize how accurate that was until you said the words."

Her smile beamed. "So you think of me as a close friend as well?"

"I think the closest I've ever had. Is that sad?"

"Not at all! I think of you as the closest female friend I've ever had. Outside Sparrow, Miels, and Tristan, I didn't have many friends."

Killian, who was seated on a cushion bench beside the mirror, scoffed. It was a common noise from the man any time Miels was mentioned, and it made Atiana have to bite the inside of her cheek from wanting to laugh every time.

But then Atiana felt the tears edge her eyes once more, and she blinked them away, looking anywhere but at the daughter of the only man she's ever wanted.

"Atiana! What did I say?" Rosaelia gasped.

"Nothing," she whispered. How cruel a joke this world

was playing on her. To make her feel closest to the Princess, the one raised by the man of her dreams, and to make that man of her dreams want nothing more than orgasms from her.

Those dark eyes he always had for her sprang to mind and stayed there.

"Please, tell me." Rosaelia stepped off her spot on the pedestal, still holding Atiana's hands as they stood a foot apart.

"Can I ask you something?" Atiana's eyes were dry once more as she stood up taller.

"Of course. Anything."

"How would you have felt if Killian had only wanted you as his whore?"

Killian's head snapped up from the knife he'd been sharpening as Rosaelia's eyes widened. The man narrowed his gaze as he paid attention to them, but Atiana turned back to the Princess.

It took her a moment to pull out of the shock, then her cheeks pinked as she looked at the closed door to Atiana's suite where they were currently working out of. "To be honest with you, At, that was kind of how we started."

"He asked you to be his whore?"

"No!" she snapped. "No, of course not. I... kinda... did." Before Atiana could say anything, she quickly explained herself. "I was in the Island, and I figured anything that happened there would be left there. It would be a perfect time to explore sexuality without the North finding out. It wasn't something I had gone there thinking would happen, but then I met Kill, and it's what I wanted. It was only going to be sex... until it wasn't."

"So you had already been together when you fell in love?"

"Yes." She smiled as if lost in memory.

A glance in the barbarian's direction showed his smile around those two scars as he watched his wife.

Atiana cleared her throat. "Okay. What if that hadn't been the case though? What if you'd fallen for him, then he asked you to be his whore? Do you think you'd do it?"

Rosaelia took a moment to truly think about it, then her brows furrowed. "No. I don't think I could. It would hurt too much knowing I was falling even more each time he touched and kissed me, and he was only using me to come."

Again, her cheeks pinked at the words, but she spoke them confidently. Probably because they were in the privacy of the suite with only people she trusted around.

"Maybe that's why we find a spirit in one another. I feel the same."

Rosaelia eyed her intently for a long minute before she seemed to realize what Atiana was speaking of. "I did not realize you love anyone."

She shrugged. "It does not matter. I will not be his whore."

There was a question there, and Atiana knew she wanted to know who this man was. She certainly wouldn't be saying, and she realized she wouldn't say anything had this not been his daughter too. It was too heart-wrenching, and she did not need her friends fighting for her or freezing with the presence of the man.

After long moments of silence, Rosaelia dropped one of Atiana's hands and used it to stroke her hair. It almost reminded Atiana of her father's hand stroking her cheek just that morning and made her want to cry all over again.

"How about this," the Princess finally said. "How about you come over tonight and we have a night just us girls? I'll invite Gem, Eve, and Etel too."

Spend more time with her? More time with both daughters? More time with other members of the Posse?

She shouldn't. It would only hurt more if they were wrenched from her life.

But she couldn't think like that. He had already stomped all over her heart. She wouldn't allow him to control her relationship with the first set of true friends she'd ever had. She loved these girls and knew they felt the same for her, knew the twins especially would deliver hell to their father's door if they found out it was he who had propositioned her.

It was time to move on, and though she didn't see herself moving on to another man, she could move on with her life.

"I'd love that."

CHAPTER 10

EDMUND

They were in the grand hall, the one only ever used for balls.

The doors were shut with only his magicians council and the two Masters within. The other members of the Posse would be coming by soon in order to help with ideas and preparations, but for now, it was only the seven of them.

Sparrow had stated he wanted the palace to find out before it became public knowledge. That would then aid them in the gossip mills sending positive things around about the situation, given Evony was a favored member at the palace. Plus, it was a good idea. They lived together. It would obviously make the most sense for those within the palace to know before the world did.

"We will need to make this a common event so we cannot put focus on you lot as royals," Aliyev spoke, circling the room. "The more blended in you are, the more everyone will be excited about the news."

Yes. That was the crux of their idea pitching at the moment. How exactly should they blend in?

"You will, however, need to break apart and hold every-one's attention to announce it," Yarro commented.

"I think we should just act as if this is one of those balls I've been told of when there're bad storms. Sparrow said everyone gathers and celebrates?" Evony stated.

"Yes, but it is not always the senior members who join," Vardan stated.

"And even if we did, it was normally in the middle of the event so attention wasn't held on us," Sparrow reminded her. "Miels and Tristan used to come in and dance but they'd dress the same as the other guards and stick with them so less atten-tion was placed on *who* they were."

"It will be different given we're there from the beginning, yes," Evony glanced around as if she was imagining it. "But if we laugh and talk with everyone, then they'll come out of their shells. We'll have others around like Miels and Tristan used to do to make us blend in more."

"That seems like an easier solution," Aliyev stated. "Who would you have around you?"

"You lot, to begin." Edmund grinned.

Asha rolled her eyes. "If we must."

Honor shimmered in her eyes as Aliyev asked with his own smirk, "Who else?"

"The guards with Tristan and the group now," Sparrow added.

"Ashtyn and Gabriel themselves, with Dale and Papa Ignatius, Papa Iskan, and Mama Beni," Evony added. "Atiana and Odolf. They're all members who would be trusted around the ball already as peers, and they're people we trust. We can spend time with them. Almost act like we're new, and they must take us around."

Edmund nodded. "Plus, from what I've been told, the magicians Gabriel found, the Cousins, at least one, if not all of them, have already attached themselves to a guard. It will help that our guards who are trusted around the palace are showcasing and falling in love with these magicians."

Yarro nodded. "Indeed. It'll be a brilliant break. From before the ball, everyone will be speaking of the Cousins because of their magician status. There will be a ton of focus on them that most might forget they're around the Lenoir line as well."

Asha nodded. "It will be a perfect warm-up for the magician announcement."

"Are we thinking of announcing her heirhood and magician hood at the same time?" Yarro asked.

"I think it would be best," Aliyev answered. "To allow all the shock to process at the same time. Plus, the Princess thing won't be much of a shock. If anything, you'll likely have muttering of people winning bets within the crowd. It is the magician part we need to make sure is sandwiched in there."

"Agreed," Sparrow stated. They were all standing toward one side of the room, but Sparrow was leaning against a wall rather than partaking in walking around, and he looked as broody and intimidating as ever as he tracked his wife's movements.

"What are we agreeing to?" Miels's voice echoed through the empty space as he opened one of the double doors to allow himself and Etel and Gemma in.

"Where's James?" Evony asked.

Gemma rolled her eyes. "You know he doesn't care for this stuff."

Evony smirked. "And you simply allowed him off?"

The Southern girl smirked back. "I allowed him to rest because I need his stamina up tonight."

Both girls threw their heads back, laughing as the magicians council turned pink. Edmund himself couldn't believe he'd gotten used to their words already but hearing them constantly speak like that all year, he now found it endearing that they were so open with their emotions.

Evony turned to her husband. "Maybe you should go rest too."

Sparrow smirked back, a dark look in his eyes. "My stamina's more than you can handle, love."

Edmund cleared his throat loudly, and conversation turned back to the ball with Yarro and Asha explaining what they'd been thinking to the newcomers.

Edmund took this moment he should've been paying attention to the group to watch the two Masters.

Evony had gone back toward her husband, and he'd opened his arms for her to snuggle in. Their foreheads leaned together—Sparrow really having to lean down to do so—as they whispered to one another, not hiding a single emotion they felt for one another. Her hands traveled his chest, but it didn't look seductive, but rather like she found serenity within him. His own hands kneaded at her hips and lower back—both because he wanted to touch her, but likely also to relieve some pain from the pregnancy.

Then Sparrow closed his eyes and leaned up to kiss her forehead, and another wave of jealousy smacked Edmund. Oh, how he'd love to give Atiana those reassuring kisses to the forehead.

He cleared his throat softly and forced himself to look away and back to the others.

EVERYTHING WAS on the right track. Plans for bringing magicians back. Plans for presenting Evony. Ending this plague. Collection of complaints around the North. Talks with the Southern council. Talks with the Island. Everything.

Everything except...

His heart banged. He loved his group, loved that they'd all found love, but that afternoon had been a lot. All of the couples were so in love with one another, so unNorthern in showing their affections, and though Edmund was happy for all of them, he was envious.

So.

Very.

Envious.

Maybe that was why he was stalking the corridors around the palace in search of the one woman who could ease him. He wouldn't get near her, wouldn't speak with her. He would stand back and discreetly watch her like he had for so many years.

It'd become a sick obsession almost five years ago when he'd gone through multiple injuries and found himself searching for her every time. It was now his custom—he needed to see her daily, even if no one was ever the wiser.

She was different this year. She was so much more... open? She was broadening her skills and spending time with more than the tailors and some servants.

He was proud of her for it, but it certainly made her more difficult to find.

He moved through the tailor's wing with the excuse of looking for Odolf whom he knew was two towns away, to the remedies room where he made an excuse for more gut health vials, to the training rooms where he simply watched the men as he passed, to the kitchens were he grabbed a handful of crisps, to the library where he pretended the book he wanted wasn't around, to the servants halls where he pretended he was making rounds.

Frustrated that he had no idea how to find her, he decided the stables were his next best option even though he was almost certain she only rode Absko in the mornings until Gabriel was back to give her lessons. A smirk was still brought to his lips at the thought.

She chose Absko.

She always chose Absko.

And he chose her.

Just like Edmund, his horse was enamored.

And he was especially glad the woman waited for Gabriel for her lessons. Out of all the help at the palace, he was the one Edmund had to worry least about. The man was too far gone for his healer.

Edmund's frown deepened when he didn't see her at the stables, making his way back to the covered outdoor corridor to circle the greens.

Then he heard it.

That sound, one he'd recognize even if he lost all of his memories. The most heavenly laugh in the world.

Edmund turned the corner, heart racing with not only the chance to see her but the opportunity to hear more of her laughs.

Then stopped abruptly.

Atiana was there, down the greens, and she was laughing.

But she wasn't alone. She wasn't with her friends. She wasn't with a female.

She was with Dale, one of the stablehands. A great man.

And they were laughing together, eyes glittering.

Hot envy ripped through his chest as Edmund stood there taking them in. They were so free, and no one would say much about a relationship between them. Matter-of-fact, it would likely be celebrated.

As Atiana turned her back to him, facing Dale and covering

whatever they were looking at, Edmund wanted to charge for them, scoop her over his shoulder and run off. What could they possibly be discussing? Her hands weren't at her sides. Were they holding hands? Were they whispering desires to one another?

His stomach rolled, bile making its way up.

Then her laugh charged through his jealous rage as her head tipped back, and Edmund knew he wouldn't move toward them. He hated it. He wanted to jump off the highest point of this palace, but this was what was best. She deserved someone as good as Dale.

And Edmund had already made a mess of their relationship by calling her his whore.

He scoffed. Of course he would never make her his whore, but having her believe it made it easier to stay away from her because *she* stayed away too, avoided his eyes half the time. He still caught himself mesmerized by those instances she didn't look away, but still, things were a little easier.

This though, watching her laugh with a male that Edmund himself approved of, was heart-wrenching.

And still, like a masochist, Edmund leaned back against the wall and watched them.

She ended up turning back, so he could see her face once more. Her smile wasn't as large as he'd seen in the past, but it was still there. She didn't reach for him, but that didn't mean anything. In the North, it wasn't uncommon to be in a relationship and not show it much in public. It was only his Posse who ignored that upbringing.

Dale watched her unabashedly, listening to her intently and smiling constantly. He didn't hide any bit of feeling, and Atiana had a way of attracting affection. Her physical beauty brought people in, but it was her internal beauty that kept everyone around. It was that internal loveliness that made Edmund's own daughters love the woman.

And as they spoke, neither of them noticed they were being watched.

They began walking away, on their way toward a set of doors at the other edge of the palace, never once noticing the King.

Edmund watched them until they were out of sight, forcing himself not to follow. Atiana deserved a happy life, and though it killed him, he would not take away her chances with Dale.

With her gone, Edmund trudged in the opposite direction toward his suite. In moments such as these, he wished alcohol had been a larger part of Northern customs. They didn't have any at the palace, and though he wasn't a drinker, he wished for the numbness that came with the burning dark liquid.

Especially if he was going to have to watch her with another man for the rest of his life.

CHAPTER II
ATIANA

It'd been just over three weeks since she'd tasted him.

Three days since they'd last spoken.

Three days of rolling through every emotion available to the human body. She had begun and ended with anger.

Her current anger was so very different from her previous ones though. Now, she was more annoyed. Before she'd been more hurt.

Annoyed, though. So very annoyed. That made her angrier with him.

The big, dumb oaf. How could he kiss her, push her against the wall and make her come against his thigh, look at her like he was going to do so again any time they passed one another, then... those words. The first set that had made her heart hurt because he was trying to protect her. The ones that had made her think he was a sweet, dumb oaf. How could he decide for her that he was no good? He might've been King, but she had half a mind to remind him that he couldn't control everything, least of all her feelings.

Then those other words.

She still couldn't believe she'd had courage enough to basically demand he give them a chance, but alas, those words had ended such desires. It'd been nearly three days and in that time, she had plenty of time between working and spending time with the girls, but also with Sparrow and James who had decided they would train her with Rosaelia, to distract her. It was a blessing, though still not enough to take the memory away entirely.

Tell me you'll spread your legs for me, and I will.

He would.

Make her his whore.

His whore!

She was seated in her suit, working, as she settled back on anger. These last few weeks since that kiss and that orgasm were beginning to affect Atiana's mind. That was the only explanation as to why she was singing such annoying children's songs at the moment. But somehow, they were the only ones that kept her sane enough to think about the big oaf—because that was something that was impossible to stop from doing—and still get work done.

With it being the start to the winter months, Atiana was as busy as all the other tailors preparing garments and accessories to keep everyone in the villages near the palace, and if they had time, further up as well, warm. The ones for palace residents had been finished for a few weeks now, Atiana as thankful as all the other tailors they were able to convince all the members to get their things done ahead of time.

As she watched the fabric slide under the sewing machine for this throw blanket she hoped reached a group of siblings, her lips tipped up in a sad smile. She wanted children of her own to make blankets like these for, to watch as they all huddled together beneath it, to make them a larger one so they could create a fort in their bedrooms and giggle together when they were meant to be sleeping.

But she only wanted them with one man, and he already had children. Grown, closer to Atiana's age, children.

Atiana made herself forget that and lived in the fantasy instead.

She imagined he hadn't said such gross words to her, and envisioned herself carrying three or maybe four all close in age, though if she went off of his bloodline, she may become pregnant only two times and end up with four children. Her lips twisted up even more, showing teeth with her smile.

The visions she'd been living with for years now had them in boy-girl order, having a son first, then a daughter, then another boy. Then, and only if they reached four, another daughter. She knew it was ludicrous to live in those thoughts considering even if she could have his babies, she had no way of determining what they'd be, but Atiana allowed herself the ease such thoughts brought her, especially in these moments of great work.

And especially when thoughts of him weren't very favorable at the moment.

But in this imagining, they would be four more Lenoirs to add to the bloodline, four more heirs to follow their sisters. Atiana didn't wish for any of her children to hold the crown, Princess Rosaelia being an amazing candidate for the role, but that wouldn't mean everyone else would not criticize her for it, say she was only trying to get the crown for herself, like the last Queen. Based on what they said about Etel, she could only imagine far worse things would be said about her.

Not that she cared.

They could talk of her for the rest of her life if she got to go to the King's wing at the end of the day—because she would have no need for a Queen's wing since this would only happen under a love match. She wished to only ever end her days kissing her husband while they watched their rascals run around the suite after one another.

Her throat closed at the vision. She wanted it more than she ever cared to explain now that the possibility had been within reach.

But that didn't mean he wanted it.

She wasn't even sure how much he wanted her. Had it only ever been a desire for her body? If so, she hated that she still wanted only him to take her virtue.

And even if he wanted her, how serious could he possibly be about breeding her? He was about to become a grandfather. Would he want to have children with her knowing he would have grandchildren older than his own children?

Atiana finished sewing the end and tied off the piece before holding it out to take a look at as she came to the conclusion of such answers in her mind—it didn't matter. This was all figments of her imagination because he'd already made it clear he only wanted her as his whore.

The blanket was a lovely wash of blues and greens with sprinkles of reds thrown in. Its reversed side was as soft as some of the animals in their farms, and the thing was large enough for two adults or four to five children to cuddle beneath.

Atiana laughed to herself as she whispered so low, it was nearly inaudible, "My King, if you weren't such a jackass, I'd suggest we get under this throw this very moment."

She was still laughing to herself as she folded the thing, wondering if this distance was hurting him as much as it hurt her. She hoped so. Hoped it hurt him more. Hoped it ripped his heart apart, made it impossible to continue living the way he'd become accustomed to.

Atiana paused. She was being a bit cruel. She still loved him, jackass or not.

As she settled the thing into the large basket of ready throws, Atiana grabbed for more fabric, this time deciding to switch over to a pair of gloves, one she could imagine putting on her little five-year-old son who looked exactly like his daddy.

She was a giddy mess with those imaginings that when the door to her suite opened, she had to fight the large grins away. She didn't need everyone questioning her about a relationship that hadn't happened.

Rose, one of the tailors she worked closely with, walked in while her two best friends, Dorothy and Blanche, stayed by the door.

"Would you mind, At, if I left these here? Sophia has decided to rearrange our suite and we do not need anything happening to these and the tailor's suite is already full," she asked, lugging a large basket of ready garments into the room.

"Of course!" Atiana pointed to the spot beside her basket, then teased, "What does Sophia not enjoy now?"

Sophia was Dorothy's mother, and all four of them shared a suite at the other end of this wing.

Rose shrugged. "I haven't a clue what goes on in that woman's head."

Atiana chuckled to herself as Rose moved the basket to its spot, rummaging through the things within to take a final look. In the meantime, Atiana couldn't help but hear what the other girls were saying.

"Mother and I saw the whole thing!" Dorothy exclaimed. "He fell! They called for the Posse healer—thank the lords she got back yesterday—and got him to his suite, but I'm not sure—"

Atiana froze, but she didn't take her eyes off the fabrics in her hands.

"But he's the King!" Blanche exclaimed. "And a bloody good one at that. We cannot lose him. I'm sure we won't."

"How?" Dorothy crossed her arms.

Atiana was so caught on holding her breath to keep herself sane in front of the women that she didn't even care if her act of being busy was lost. They were speaking of Edmund. What could've possibly happene—

"He's in his forties. Don't you think he's been stung by an Alomora bee before? He's made it out alive before."

An Alomora bee sting? Blanche was right. With that, Ashtyn should be able to disperse Etel's serum through his body faster and heal him completely.

But only if the girls got to him on time. Without Etel's serum, Ashtyn couldn't do a thing. Etel was vital to those with allergies in the palace, and Edmund's aversion to Alomora bees was stronger than most people's. The medics would be able to help those with less severe allergies because they had the time to make the concoctions and heal the patient, but not in these cases. In these serious cases, a remedies maker was preferred and ready-made vials required.

Atiana swallowed, her entire body jittering with the need to get these women out.

They were still talking to one another, comments and jokes being thrown, both about the King and not, but Atiana could hardly pay attention. She only barely heard Rose as she bid her farewell, and they closed the door behind them.

Only in that moment did she allow herself to exhale and all the tears she'd been trying to store come tumbling out.

Her eyes snapped to her door and she didn't care any

longer. Atiana rose and slowly moved for her door. Once in the corridor, she tried to keep calm and walk normally.

She made it nearly to the King's wing that way before she could no longer take it and began running. She didn't care how inappropriate this was, how much trouble she could get into for running into the King's wing, none of it. She just had to know he wasn't dying, that the final words she'd said to him weren't "I hate you."

CHAPTER 12

EDMUND

The only thing making him feel unwell at the moment was the chaos of all of his children—because the King looked to all of the Posse members as his children—yelling at him to get back to bed. It at least shut them up a little when he got undressed, causing the women to turn away and head out of his bedroom and into the common space. The men, though, followed him into his shower.

He wished to soak in the bathtub that sat only a few feet from his shower, but now didn't feel like the time for it. He was extremely happy in moments like these that as King, he had his own bathing chamber whereas the others of his Posse shared at the end of the hall. He loved his peace as he soaked hard days away, but as they very moment, he simply wanted to wash away the sweat that had come from his body's need to keep him alive and get out of there.

"Edmund, you're being unreasonable," Miels demanded as the King gave the men his back. "It will not kill you to lie in bed an extra day, and no one will think less of you for it."

Edmund scrubbed at his body until his skin felt brand new,

then responded, "I'm aware, boys. But I have no need to rest. I feel absolutely fine."

"Where, exactly, do you feel the need to be that you cannot simply stay in your rooms tonight?" Sparrow questioned, and as Edmund turned to glance his way, a dark look in his eyes said the Assassin had a guess.

Edmund narrowed his eyes at the man. "Do not interrogate me. I have nothing of absolute importance to deal with. I simply do not wish to be stuck in here when I do not need to be."

Sparrow huffed. "You know the girls are more relentless than us, Ed. That's not a very convincing statement."

Edmund shuffled around as he exited the shower space, the air rushing at the dampness of his body and cooling him down. He was doing everything in his power *not* to think of the destination he wished to rush to because his body was victim to react immediately to it and he didn't need the boys seeing his erection.

James handed him a towel as he stepped completely out and dried himself while moving back for his room. The door to the common space was just closing as he stepped out and a single glance around told him the girls had been in here changing his sheets to fresh ones while he was in the bath. His lips tipped up at the kindness, even if he knew they'd done so in order to make the bed appealing once more.

Edmund dressed as the boys continued trying to convince him, Tristan even holding up and dancing with a comfortable sleeping trouser which almost had the desired effect of getting him back into them. Not back to bed, but in those trousers and nothing else as he sat by the fire in his common space with a cup of tea, watching the ashes fill the hearth as if they were pieces of his heart withering away.

But now that he was dressed and his back to the boys, he

could think of the reason for his need to depart. For the past nearly seven years, but especially the past four, every time Edmund had gotten hurt in any capacity, he'd needed to see her, as if his heart could not completely settle until he saw his beautiful tailor.

Like a command to hearing her name—even if only thought in his mind—his cock hardened. He adjusted himself in his pants as he threw his shirt on and turned back for their ramblings. Edmund strolled past them on his way out of the bedroom as they continued.

Out in the common space, the women took over, Rosaelia being the loudest of all because she knew he'd listen to her above the rest of them. Too bad she wasn't aware that she wasn't the woman who controlled his actions completely.

"Father, please," she whined in that voice that had always gotten her what she wanted as a child.

He cradled her face and kissed her crown. "Relax, daughter. I am fine, and I am certainly in no mood to be lying about all day."

"It is nearly night." Evony joined her sister. "You will need to be back here soon anyway."

Edmund moved for the table beside his couch that held his little piece of cloth. He played the thing off as a handkerchief but it wasn't one. It was simply the piece of cloth Atiana had been chasing the day the two of them met. He made a point to always be carrying it. Once safe in his pocket, his hand fidgeted with it knowing he was that much closer to seeing her, angry with him or not.

"This has been exciting, children, really." He turned back for them. "But I need to g—"

Their rebuttals were stopped as the double doors to his suite came crashing open. All heads turned immediately for the intrusion, and Edmund's eyes widened.

Standing between those open doors that no one but his Posse would be allowed into at such a time, and certainly never anyone who would simply barge in, was the woman he'd been in a desperate need to get to.

And she had tears strolling down her face.

In the echoing silence, her shoulders fell, and she sighed, tears coming down harder. She looked so beautiful, he wouldn't have been able to peel his gaze away had be tried.

"You're okay," she finally whispered, and her tears seemed to tumble out even faster.

Edmund felt the energy in the room shift suddenly. He knew they were all staring between the two of them, but he only had eyes for his girl. He wanted to rush for her. The way her hands fidgeted at her sides said she wanted to come for him.

But neither of them moved.

No one moved.

Then suddenly, they were all in action. All of his children sprung out of their frozen states and rushed for the doors. Comments from all of them clouded the room. "Well, looks like you're taken care of," and "We'll leave you to it then," and "My father is the one she'd been speaking of!" and "Finally someone to put you in your place." And he swore he heard mutterings from Sparrow along the line of "At least we know now he won't be leaving the room," and Miels's response of "For a few days maybe."

Either Atiana didn't hear them as they shuffled past her and closed the doors or she didn't care. Given she'd slammed into his rooms knowing they would all be there, Edmund thought the latter.

The silence echoed around them with the Posse gone.

Atiana looked as stunning as ever. Her dark locks down her back in light waves, contouring her looks incredibly. Her inviting eyes surrounded by those thick lashes were heavenly, comforting, his.

"Atiana." His voice was hoarse as the whisper left him.

"Edmund," her lips mouthed, but it was so low, he couldn't hear his name off her lips.

His jaw ground. He loved when she said his name so rare an occasion as it was.

Then his body became hyperaware of the fact that tears continued to slowly fall down her cheeks.

That broke him out of his stance. He only took a single step forward when she gasped, charging his body into motion and speeding toward her. He had her face cradled into his hands and his lips on hers in seconds.

They both moaned into the kiss, and Edmund knew in that moment that no matter what arguments they had in the future, he could not, would not, stand being away from her any longer.

She was his.

CHAPTER 13
ATIANA

He was okay. He was okay. He was okay.

The words repeated in her mind like a mantra as their tongues brushed, his large strong hands holding her in place like he'd never let her go again.

He was slow with the kiss, passionate as he took in every second of her taste. Then he pulled away all too soon for her likings, thumbs brushing away the tears. "Stop crying, my love."

Her head shook but she couldn't say anything as her hands rushed over his form as if she didn't know he had only been stung therefore he wouldn't have any injuries.

"Atiana, my love. I'm perfectly fine, especially now." He brushed the final tears flowing down her cheeks away, then kissed her once more.

When he pulled away, his hands fell from her face to take hers into them. He rested them at his chest, and she could feel the beat of his heart underneath. It was rhythmic, calm, the complete opposite to hers.

"Wher-wher-where were you going?" She was a complete

blubbering mess. She couldn't fathom what part of this he found amusing enough to smile at.

"To find you."

Her eyes widened, and her fingers dug into his shirt. "What?"

He brought one of her hands to his lips, kissing her knuckles softly. "I need to see you every day, but especially on those days where something could've happened to me. You're my saving grace, Atiana."

"I love you," she blurted, unable to stop the words, needing him to know those final words from before had been a lie.

His chuckle was deep and dark as he dropped her hands and took her face into his hands once more. "I love you more. I'm quite literally enamored by you."

Warmth spread throughout her body as her breaths quickened. She'd waited years to hear those words, and they were as lovely as she'd expected.

She swallowed, licking her lips and tasting the salty tears. "Your family is right. You need to rest. I just... I needed to know you were all right."

He held her still. "I do not need rest. I need *you*. Stay with me."

More tears fled her eyes as her head shook without her control. "I cannot..." She squared her shoulders. "I *will not* be your whore."

He released an amused scoff. "As if I'd ever allow it."

"But you said—"

"I lied, my love. I needed you to hate me, to need me to keep my distance so it was easier for me to do so."

"You... lied?"

His thumbs brushed her bottom lip as his fingers tightened their hold on her head. "I am in love with you. I do not know everything about you, but I know I believe in love at first sight, and you have been it for me for nearly seven years, Atiana. I would never allow you to be anything more than my Queen."

She blinked as she took him in. Slowly processing his words. "You... lied?"

He chuckled. "You're so good, Atiana. You cannot always believe others."

"I don't," she whispered. "But you..." *I never want to not trust you.*

He huffed, almost as if he couldn't believe his luck. Then he leaned down and kissed her once more, softly, memorizing her lips. Atiana could not think. She could do nothing but live in this moment, in this meeting of lips she never thought she'd be able to experience again.

As their tongues moved together, Atiana was stuck between getting lost in his mouth or with the way his hands now moved down her body. They touched her everywhere, held on to her hips and slithered over her bum. They made every inch of her tingle with desire even through the layers of clothes that still separated them.

"Edmund..." Her voice was breathy. "I've never..."

His lips were on her still, slithering down her jaw and distracting the words she wanted to let out. His tongue suckled at her neck, then he bit his way up to her ear, pulling her lobe between his teeth. "Good. You belong to me, Atiana. No one else."

"What if I'm not ready?"

He pulled away abruptly. "Is that so?"

"No." She quickly corrected the one-word answer. "I mean, I want you. I've wanted you for so long, but what if I were to say no now?"

"Then I'd wait a lifetime for you, my love."

Atiana's breath caught. He wasn't lying. She knew it now, could see how different he sounded from when he'd been calling her his whore. There was something else in his eyes too, something akin to salvation.

"I love you, Edmund," she finally said. "I've waited all these years for you. I don't want to wait anymore."

That salvation shimmering in his eyes, it turned to hope, to relief, to unadulterated adoration.

Edmund stepped away and took her hands, walking backward as he led her to his bedroom. She wanted to look around, take in the common space and the bedroom given it was her first time in both, but Atiana could not take her eyes off of the man before her.

By the large bed, he released her, and to her surprise, reached for his own shirt rather than her dress. She'd been expecting him to undress her, to be in a hurry to see her bare and to own every inch of her.

But he was moving slowly.

This was her first time. He knew that now.

Atiana cleared her throat. "You do not have to be fragile with me. I can take whatever you wish to give."

Another huff of amusement passed his lips as he chucked his shirt to some corner of his room. "I have every intention of doing every depraved thing imaginable to you, my love. But we'll have a lifetime for that. Tonight, I wish to take things slow, cherish this, you."

"I will not break if we go any faster."

He smirked. "I might."

"Edmund—"

"I might absolutely combust at the sight of you naked, love. Allow me to take things slow."

Atiana breathed. She believed him. Based on the amount of control he seemed to lose when she'd touched his arm on the walk to her suite all those weeks ago, she believed he certainly might combust were they to move too quickly.

It almost made her chuckle.

As his hands pulled on the ties to his trousers, any amusement she may've had died within her. Atiana had never seen a man's penis before, and certainly never an erect one.

She swallowed as he allowed his trousers to fall and she took in his form from head to toe. He was all muscle with hair trickled over his chest, arms, thighs, his... cock. He looked every way a man, a leader, a king. Atiana was suddenly glad they were taking things slowly.

"You're quite... endowed."

Edmund completely laughed now. "Thank you."

"Do you wish for me to undress now?"

He gave a small grin. "Do you not want to?"

To her surprise, a smirk rose on her lips. "I'd prefer if you undressed me."

He swallowed. Swallowed. As if he were the virgin between them. It made her feel powerful.

Edmund stepped up to her, accepting the challenge, before hesitation took over his features and instead of reaching for the ties to the front of her dress, he sat on the edge of the bed.

"Is something the matt—"

Before she could finish her question, his hands were tight around her hips and he had her placed between his legs. "I think I'll have better control of myself seated."

Atiana giggled but allowed him free reign over her body.

His hands were steady as they pulled the ties that held her dress down, then slowly pulled at the fabric until it was loose around her chest. The index finger on either of his hands teased her as he stuck his fingers into her dress and slowly pulled down. His thumbs were quick on her nipples the moment they were free, giving them the second of chill before the warmth of his fingers replaced the feeling.

Atiana only breathed. This was so much to take in.

Edmund's fingers teased her, plucking at her nipples before taking her breasts into his large hands and kneading them. Though his hands were calloused from all the training he put himself through, they felt heavenly against her softness.

Atiana's head tipped back and her eyes closed as she enjoyed the pleasure of the air on her top half and his hands warming her.

Then her eyes shot open.

Her breasts were warm. Too warm.

Looking down, Atiana's cunt clenched in a way it never had before. Edmund had her breast in his mouth, then his gaze flickered up to her and there was mischief there as he slowly released her breast until her nipple was stuck between his teeth. He pulled. Hard. The pain was too pleasurable, and Atiana grabbed onto his shoulders to keep herself standing.

Moans passed her lips which only seemed to incentivize him more as he lapped at the opposite breast. Her nails dug in harder, her breaths came in more ragged, and yet, Edmund enjoyed himself.

It was when Atiana could no longer handle it that her hand slipped to the back of his head and she pulled on his hair with all her might. "Edmund, please."

Edmund smirked as he appeased her and began kissing down her stomach to the edge of where her dress still hung from her hips. He tugged on the fabric to drop it to the floor as he left open-mouth kisses and bite marks on her lower stomach.

"You taste divine," he whispered against her as if he could not find the power to peel his lips from her skin.

His lips continued their travel down, and Atiana gasped when his open-mouth kisses reached her most private of areas. His tongue lapped at her as his hands forced her shaky legs apart.

"Edmund," she begged. "I cannot keep standing."

He chuckled, and the vibrations felt heavenly upon her skin. "Now I feel the need to show you otherwise."

"Please," she moaned.

Edmund ignored her as his mouth moved for her cunt and he sucked her in.

Atiana gasped, her hands gripped at all of him, and her head fell back. Her knees wobbled, and she hoped that was enough proof that she would not be able to hold herself up.

Apparently, that only challenged him to *keep* her standing.

His hands slithered around her thighs and held the backs so even if she were to fall, he'd keep her standing. The sight of his veiny arms only made her cling to him harder.

His tongue was like hot liquid as it slithered through her slit, awakening a part of her that felt liable to combust as well. If this was what he felt every time she simply touched him, she could not fathom how he'd had the power to control himself at all.

That feeling burned the space beneath her skin. All of her. It spread and burned and grew hotter still the closer it got to her core.

As she cried out his name over and over again, Atiana stopped caring about holding herself up and allowed all of her weight to fall into his hands. As he feasted, the feeling became too much. She would truly combust.

"Edmund, I can't. It's too much. Edmund, I—" she moaned before her words became intelligible and she exploded.

She was in a cloud of darkness with stars alight everywhere. She was part of everything and nothing, weightless and everlasting.

Atiana didn't know how long it took before she came down from the feeling, but when she finally did, she realized she hadn't exploded. She'd come. She'd never experienced anything quite so all-encompassing.

When she could finally find it in herself to move again, she simply looked down to where Edmund was watching her. He looked in awe as he took in her every emotion.

"My Queen, Atiana. You are it."

She could not find breath enough to speak quite yet but she found strength to lift off of his hands and push at his shoulders until he took the hint to lie back.

Edmund grinned with a sexy look in his eyes as he not only laid back, but also slithered higher up the bed. "Would you like to sit on my face now?"

With what lit bit of energy she'd mustered, Atiana crawled onto the bed and began prowling between his spread legs. "I want you to take me now." She kissed his legs, slowly switching as she made her way higher.

When she reached his cock, Atiana only planned on kissing it like she had his legs before making her way higher, but the urge to open her mouth and taste him was too great.

She had the tip of his large length in her mouth when his hand landed in her hair with a gasp. "Atiana, what are you doing?"

Catching his features from between her lashes, she realized why he'd ravished her so before. This power and control she felt from the things *she* did to him was all-consuming. She didn't want it to end.

Atiana slowly licked around the tip before kissing it again. "You tasted me, my King."

"I need to be inside you, Atiana," he growled.

The panic in his voice only made her want to slow down. "Good things come to those who wait, my love."

"Atiana," he demanded just before she slipped his length into her mouth again and his head fell back. "Fuck."

She could not fit all of him in her mouth, and given this was her first time, Atiana didn't find the need to try. She'd have plenty of time in the future for that. For now, she simply wanted to play with him.

Unfortunately, her games would not last long. As she twirled her tongue around his cock again, his hand tightened in her hair so harshly, she was forced to pop him out and travel up to his mouth, spit still tying her to his cock.

"Baby, later, I'm going to fuck the shit out of your mouth. But please. I need to be inside you," he gritted as if it took all of him not to throw her down and take what he wanted.

She swallowed. "Then have me, my love."

As if the words snapped a tether, he quickly pushed her to the bed and hovered over her so her world began and ended with him and only him. He forced her legs apart and held one of her hands as he allowed the other to cling to his back, then he slowly eased his cock through her wet folds.

"I'm going to breed you, Atiana. You are never going to take a tonic."

Controlling, demanding man. "As you wish."

He smirked as he slipped the tip of his cock into her cunt, then immediately slammed into her.

The sensation hurt, but she was glad he did it quickly.

He gave her only a moment to adjust in which her cunt clenched and unclenched, finding this new normal with his large intrusion.

Then he was making love to her. Slow, passionate, gaze filled with the love she now *knew* he felt as deeply as she did.

"I love you, Atiana. I never wish to be parted from you. I cannot bare it." Each statement came with another thrust, and each time, Atiana dug him in closer.

"I'm yours. From this day forward, I belong to you," she

promised as if she hadn't belonged to him for the last seven years.

He kissed her, matching the pace of his thrusts.

It was all too much. Too much intensity, too much heat, too much love. Atiana could no longer handle it.

"Edmund, I'm going to..."

"Me too," he grunted. "Me too, my love."

His thrusts moved deeper, and Atiana broke at the sound of his groans as he came within her.

As she came, she watched him through her slitted eyes and knew her love story was finally starting.

CHAPTER 14
EDMUND

Edmund's muscles had been massaged thoroughly before. As King, he'd had the best of the best push out the pains he'd gained while training. And still, nothing he'd ever experienced before compared to how lax his body was lying in bed next to the most beautiful woman he'd ever seen.

It'd been nearly impossible to pull himself out of bed, and even then, he hadn't been able to do it without tasting her again. She'd woken with those breathy moans and her half-lidded eyes had found him feasting between her thighs.

After tasting her cum on his tongue, Edmund had moved up her pliant body and kissed her good morning, his cock throbbing more when she kissed him back feverishly, tasting herself all over his tongue.

Then he'd fucked her.

Harder than the night before.

She'd drained him of everything when her walls had squeezed with her orgasm and he'd come inside her.

Then it'd been *really* difficult to leave, but she'd made it a little easier by reminding him that she wouldn't be staying in bed either.

Together they'd bathed, then gotten dressed.

And now, he was going to meet his boys.

He'd always loved time training with them. Always. But for the first time—ever—it wasn't the most exciting thing.

Because of his busier schedule now that he was so focused on allowing magicians back into the North, Edmund didn't have the same bouts of freedom to train with them as he'd had before. He still took advantage of Sparrow's mornings, so he never went without, but there was something about training will all of his boys that beat that.

Though Tristan wasn't around.

James and Killian had taken up the space, but things wouldn't feel complete until his second spy was back with them. Though he loved everyone in the Posse, Edmund held a special connection to his three boys.

Currently, they were broken into two groups of two with Sparrow sitting out the match. Killian would be joining Edmund against James and Miels as they practiced being on the offensive and defensive in a "real life" situation where multiple swords could be coming down at once, and your partner may or may not be around to help.

Edmund was blocking and defending blows from both James and Miels as Killian got more comfortable with his weapon given swords weren't used in the Island Nation but his attention snagged once again to Sparrow speaking to Dale off by the weapons table. He maneuvered his steps so he was closer to them in order to hear what they were discussing, if Atiana came up.

"Trust me, I understand you a lot more now than I ever have," Dale responded to something Sparrow had said. "Love is..." He shook his head. "I shouldn't have made fun of Gabriel for it so much."

Sparrow smirked. "And are you being as discreet with your feelings as Gabriel always has been."

Cling, cling, cling, swords clashed against one another as Killian pushed their opposition to the other end of the mats, away from the boys' conversation.

Fuck!

Edmund moved with them, only catching the beginning of Dale's words, "About as much, but she told me..."

"Are you distracted today, our almighty one?" Miels smirked while bringing his sword down hard.

Edmund caught the hit, his arm straining at the pressure before he pushed the boy away. "Maybe your King wishes for you to believe that to make this win so much easier."

Both James and Miels laughed as they charged with more aggression, Killian doing spectacularly at blocking them given his limited training with the weapon. He was a very fast study, and Edmund knew he'd had his own private trainings with Sparrow to get there quicker.

Edmund took the moment to step away from the fight and take in his boys. Killian, the savage that he was, spent much of his time with the hunters since he'd grown up hunting and enjoyed it above all else, but he'd also taken his responsibility as the future Queen's husband seriously. He trained in every way—physically, with weapons, whether swords or daggers or arrows; intellectually, learning all the laws and histories of the North; and socially, figuring out what would be needed of him as future King. That last one was his most difficult as the man was the farthest thing from a people person.

Before him, James had been his newest man as Evony's best friend, he'd only come into the group when Edmund found out he had a second daughter. He'd gotten so close to Tristan and Miels in the process, Miels especially now, that it was difficult to picture his spies as a duo any longer. They were more of a trio, though unlike the two spies, James's skin, hair, and eyes were all darker.

And with James came Gemma, only about a month more pregnant than Evony. Edmund was glad the best friends would be having children together, and he could not help his heart palpitations at the reality of two grandbabies soon. Though neither Gemma nor James were related to him, like the other boys of the Posse, their children would be like family to Edmund. It was only a couple of months away.

Miels pushed Killian back, bringing Edmund back into the fight, and once again the two were working them back so Edmund would be able to hear more of the conversation at the other end.

"...Atiana's the most beautiful."

Fury like he'd never felt before raged through Edmund's chest, and it took everything in him not to turn the sword around on the stablehand. Of course he thought Atiana was the most beautiful. Everyone did.

"Yes, I've been thinking of asking her for one too," Sparrow answered, and Edmund was momentarily confused at the turn of conversation. "After Evony gives birth, I think she'd like an especially nice pair of trousers."

"That's a good point actually. Amara might not want a dress. Fuck. I already told Atiana a dress, but she lives and works in Kent. She might prefer trousers and a vest."

Kent? Their neighboring town? Dale was speaking of a woman from Kent? He was speaking of Atiana as a tailor, not a lover. He'd been referring to Atiana's most beautiful designs.

Thank the lords.

"Have you two discussed whether she would move here?

Or were you planning on leaving the palace?" Sparrow asked as he sharpened a sword by the table, his back now to the mats making it more difficult to hear their conversation.

"Call it!" Miels barked and they all stopped fighting, thankfully pausing the clash of swords and making eavesdropping far simpler, as he moved to the side of the room where his wife was waiting for him as if she eagerly needed to tell him something.

Edmund's lips tipped up at the two as they stood close to one another to whisper their secrets as he listened back in on the two men behind him.

"I would do anything she desired. I think she might like the palace but if she decides she'd rather stay in Kent, I'll be moving to Kent. I want to marry her as soon as she'd allow me to. I want her pregnant."

Sparrow barked a laugh. "So you understand now."

Edmund scoffed internally. *He* understood now. He'd understood for a long time now, wanting nothing more for years than to get Atiana pregnant, but now that he'd truly tasted her, been inside her, he *needed* to breed her.

Satisfied that Dale was speaking of another female and he had nothing to worry about, Edmund stopped listening in and instead allowed his thoughts to turn back to his future Queen. He needed to marry her. Soon. Like Dale, he didn't want to wait.

And given Atiana could already be pregnant from when he'd come inside her, he wanted it done as soon as yesterday.

Killian brought him out of his thoughts, sweat drenching his shirt everywhere like it was on Edmund. "Your balance when you blocked Miels's outward blow, where did your weight stand?"

Edmund grinned, remembering a time when he had three

little boys asking him all sorts of training questions before they became better than him, and turned to give Killian all the instruction he wanted.

CHAPTER 15
EDMUND

After the work they'd put on the mats battling one another in multiple rounds, whether offensive or defensive, then the technical trainings and conditioning in between each round, Edmund and his boys had been drenched on every inch of their bodies. They'd scurried together to the men's bathing chamber in the King's wing. Though Edmund had his own in his quarters, he'd been having such a nice day with his boys that he didn't want to cut it short, and he certainly didn't want to draw attention to their stations, as if he was somehow better because he was King.

They continued their loud conversations regarding different battles they'd each been in while showering in steaming waters that made Edmund glad he'd afforded everyone in the North the ability to have. Then they continued those exuberant talks to his suite where everyone found a spot in the common space and rested their bodies.

Edmund felt great. Sore like he'd never believe but great. Though the shower had helped, he knew nothing would feel better than to pump into a certain beauty until he'd released into her at least twice.

His head fell back at the simple thought of being within her again. He'd become addicted. This was why he'd stayed away, kept a cold stare any time they were near one another. He'd tasted her, felt her, and there was no going back. He felt fucking possessed.

"If Eve wasn't pregnant, she could show you the skill she possesses when she fights with her magic," James told the others. "It's unbelievable."

Sparrow let out a sound from the back of his throat in agreement.

Miels smirked at the man. "Unbelievable enough to beat you too, Mr. Assassin?"

"I would never fight my wife. If she wants to raise a sword at me, the world can say goodbye to the Master Assassin."

James made a whipping sound, and they all broke out into laughter.

Sparrow rolled his eyes being the only one not laughing. "Please. I've *seen* your wife put a dagger to your throat."

James's head fell back in memory. "Yes. Her hormones are... heightened."

Killian smirked. "Both women's are. They're going to be giving birth to some aggressive ones if what I've been told is correct and they're normally sweet."

Both Sparrow and James smirked, eyes beaming like the proud fathers they were soon to be.

Edmund remembered learning of Rowena's pregnancy twenty-one years ago. He remembered the sting of fear that raced through him and the months it took for apprehension to turn. It didn't. Not until baby Rosaelia was brought to him by the nurse maids and he'd looked into those beautiful green eyes. It still stung remembering he should've held two daughters that day, but there was no changing the past.

Looking out at the two men, he was glad apprehension had hardly played a role with them. They'd both instantly been excited, then overly protective.

That was another thing. He had others take care of Rowena to make sure nothing happened to his heir—because though he'd been apprehensive, he knew he'd love his child—but he had never been protective of her. They hadn't been a love match, but Edmund had respected his wife back then. Yet still, he hadn't cared about being overly protective of her.

If it hadn't been for Atiana, he didn't think he'd ever understand what the other men in this room did. He wanted to protect Atiana against any and every thing, and he knew the moment he found out she was carrying his child, he would be worse than Sparrow was with Evony.

"Yes," Miels huffed. "Our sweet girls turn more into monsters now. Scarier than anything I've been against."

That got smiles from everyone as Killian responded, "I can imagine. Women have that talent."

"Which one is that?" James asked.

"Being scarier than their counterparts. Even while not raging with pregnancy hormones."

All of the men looked to one another, excitement brimming at any story the barbarian would share with them. It was difficult to believe he, who had survived horrendous times, could find women, ones as sweet and small as the ones they kept around, frightening.

"And do you have an example of such an occasion?" Edmund asked.

"Of course," Killian remarked, sitting back. "Nor and I had been about twelve at the time." Though Norya was the tallest and toughest of their women, even she was small compared to all the men in the Posse. "We'd gone out to hunt because we were bored and it was spring and nice out—though I imagine still much colder than your springs here—and we came upon this cat. I still don't know what kind it was. We never found one like it. Nor was scary when she—" He sat up. "I need to get to my wife before she rages at me."

They all blinked at the sudden comment as James asked. "What?"

Killian nodded at the timepiece in the corner of the room. "I'm meant to meet with Sael now. If I'm late, she'll rage, and that'll be another story to add to my catalog."

Everyone laughed, and Edmund loved seeing that his daughter had someone who was a little afraid of her wrath. He should be. All men should be afraid of their woman's wrath.

As if that was bringing the wonderful afternoon to an end, everyone got up with him, leaving the suite to likely rest a little before dinner, and Edmund followed them out to hear the end of Killian's tale.

"Anyway, it had been so much larger than what you could expect from a cat species, but you would think it was the size of a hare the way Nor sauntered past it. About as big as me, it took the both of us to carry it—barely—after Nor killed it. I realized then that women must be scarier than men."

They all laughed as they walked out of Edmund's suite right as Rosaelia's door opened and a cacophony of female noises came out. Rosaelia turned in their direction and her smile broadened. "Right on time, barbarian."

Edmund refused to look in the man's direction, almost certain there was a heated look in his eyes as he followed her into their suite. "I'm sore, princess. Can I get your mouth to relax me?"

Edmund shivered at the thought of his daughter doing anything to him with her mouth, but turned his gaze instead on a certain tailor standing around the other women who were being embraced by their men.

As he stood there taking in the woman he was in love with, surrounded by the most important people in his life, Edmund couldn't fathom anything feeling more right than this. She was meant to be there with them. It was clear as day. And as the thoughts flooded him, another set of shivers ran through Edmund's entire form. One that he knew accompanied a heated look.

CHAPTER 16
ATIANA

Atiana was blushing. She knew it but she could not stop it.

From the words being spoken by all the men to their women around her to the hungry look Edmund was throwing her way, she was surprised she hadn't combusted in the middle of that hall.

Edmund smirked as if he knew what was happening to her, then held out his hand, beckoning her from the throng of people around the hall. She obeyed without thought.

With her hand in his, Edmund brought her in close until their bodies were pressed together and he had his other hand wrapped around her waist. "I've missed you."

Her blush deepened. "You saw me this morning. You were... *in* me this morning." She whispered that last bit.

Edmund chuckled into her ear. "Are you sore?"

"A little bit." She stared at his shirt.

He released her hand and tipped her chin up instead. "Would you like me to kiss it better for you?"

Atiana was the color of a tomato. She knew it. "Aren't you

sore? All of the men were telling their women they were sore. Your training took a while today."

He smirked, and Atiana was glad for the arm around her waist, for her knees turned to mush immediately. "You can kiss me better later if you'd like. I want to make you come first. On my tongue, then my cock, then we can visit your kisses."

"Edmund," she hissed, given he hadn't whispered that statement and there were others around.

He chuckled, deep and proud, as he began walking backward, pulling her with him. "Relax, my love. They're all too busy with their own meals to listen to us."

Meals.

Lords, she was surely to combust.

With the doors to Edmund's suite closed, he wasted no time tugging at the ties of her dress to pull the fabric off her shoulders. His lips pressed to the skin as he slipped the fabric lower, down her chest until it sat at her hips. "You smell so lovely. Add that to your taste, and it will become impossible to peel myself out of bed in the mornings." He kissed behind her ear as his hands fisted at the fabric around her waist and tugged at it until it fell to the ground.

He lifted his head to look at her and for a moment, it was pure affection and not lust that stared down at her. Atiana's heart leaped. She'd thought herself in love before, but it felt stronger now. Was this how it would be? Affection that grew with each passing day? She could not fathom loving him more than she already did.

"Everything about you was made for me, my love."

She gave a small smile. "Yes. All of me. It's yours."

He leaned in and kissed her lips before pulling away and moving her to the couch. He eased her down in the corner by the fire, and she was thankful for it because though her body burned with desire, the heat would help with the cold that seeped into the palace from time to time.

Standing before her, Edmund removed his shirt then his trousers so his hard cock bobbed before her face. Atiana licked her lips, but she wasn't given the opportunity to taste him as he lowered to his knees.

Spreading her legs so his body fit between them, he leaned in closer and kissed her with vigor, his tongue sweeping into her mouth and taking her hostage.

Atiana's hands wrapped around his shoulders, nails raking over skin she'd fantasized about for years.

"Did you have a nice day?" he asked as he kissed down her jaw.

"Mmhm."

He took her ear into his mouth and sucked. "That's all? Is it a secret meeting you girls have?"

She wasn't sure if actual words came past her lips as he moved down to her neck.

He chuckled as he kissed every inch of her neck. "Did you talk about me?"

"Mmhm." She tugged on his shoulders to bring him closer.

"Of course. My daughters are the nosiest women I've ever met."

"Edmund," she moaned as he lowered his open-mouthed kisses to her chest.

"You're right." He smiled against her skin as his tongue flicked over a nipple. "That's enough talk of them." He flicked his tongue against her other nipple, then sucked her into his mouth.

She knew she enjoyed his mouth on her breasts from the night before, but never would she have imagined so much pleasure simply from his tongue and teeth tasting her breasts.

Pressure began at her core, and Atiana didn't know whether it was possible, but she was sure she was going to come.

Atiana never wanted this to end. Her cunt clenched with need, but she was too lost in the feel of his mouth sucking at her breasts. She breathed his name, thanked the lords, maybe even muttered a few curse words. She wasn't entirely in charge of what was happening to her mouth.

"Fuck," Edmund hissed, bringing Atiana out of her clouds as she opened her eyes and glanced down. "I may have gotten a bit carried away."

He was staring at her breasts which were now covered in hickeys and bite marks. He looked almost mesmerized as he took them in, as if he'd created a piece of art before he flicked his tongue over one of her nipples.

She moaned softly. "I like them. I like having evidence on my body that we were together."

He flickered her nipple again before quickly sucking and biting on it, then he kissed softly down her stomach. "That's good, my love." His gaze flickered up to her as his shoulders spread her legs even wider. "Because I plan on leaving a lot more."

She blushed, excited for what he'd do to her as his mouth descended on her inner thighs and he began to bite and suck there.

Atiana's back arched as her head fell back, her eyes fluttering closed as unabashed moans left her. Pressure continued to build low in her stomach like it had when he'd been enjoying her breasts. It was unfathomable, but she knew it was going to happen—she was going to come without his touching her cunt.

Her fingers fell into his hair as she writhed beneath him, and yet, he still stayed away from her cunt. He tasted her arousal on her thighs though. She was so wet that her thighs would stick together if he allowed them to close.

"Edmund," she moaned. "Edmund... I'm going to..." Her back arched, but he didn't stop sucking on the inside of her thigh, staring up to meet her half-open eyes with a glimmer of mischief within his dark orbs.

She pulled on his hair as she came, breathing his name like a prayer.

"My, my, Atiana. That pussy is going to be soaking when my tongue touches it now."

She whimpered, her inner walls clenching at the thought of him finally touching her where she needed him.

He chuckled, still watching her intently as he lowered his face, his hands holding her thighs apart, likely hard enough to leave fingerprints. She couldn't wait to look at herself in the mirror later. He would be all over her.

He growled as his tongue took its first lap up her slit causing her back to arch, wanting to get her cunt closer to his face as if there was any more space between them.

He released one of her thighs so his fingers could tease her entrance, and Atiana's leg immediately fell over his shoulder, foot dragging down his back to get him closer.

As he licked her up and down, Atiana thrashed.

As his finger slowly slid into her opening, her body rolled.

As he sucked on her clit and fucked his finger into her, she completely lost any concept on life. She began and ended with him. Only him.

As one finger turned to two, then three, Atiana burned as she stretched, pleasure rolling through her in waves. He hooked his fingers within her, mouth constantly giving her clit the attention it required, and Atiana was lost to the orgasm ripping through her.

She called out his name. Only his name. Only able to think of that one word.

Edmund,

Edmund,

"Edmund!"

He smirked up at her as he lapped up all of her juices, fingers still moving within her. As he pulled away, his fingers slowed their movement until finally, he removed them.

He brought those three fingers up to her mouth, and Atiana wasn't in charge of her own actions as she immediately opened to suck them. All she knew was what he wanted from her, and she wanted to give him everything.

The thumb of his other hand rubbed circles into her clit as she sucked his fingers back, tasting herself. She moaned against his fingers, already prepared for the taste of his cock after she came all over it.

Finally, Edmund released his hands from her, and just as she was going to whimper, he fell onto the couch beside her, lifting her dead body up and onto his lap. She moaned as her sensitive breasts grazed the hairs on his chest.

As she held on around his shoulders, kissing and licking at his neck, Edmund guided his cock through her soaking folds before positioning himself at her opening, then his hands settled on her waist, and he slowly eased her down. "Ride me, my love. Fuck. Make yourself come on my cock. Milk me."

Atiana's head fell back at the demands as her body listened, instantly moving.

"Yes, Atiana. Milk my cock. Fill this exquisite pussy with my cum. Do a good job, and I'll eat your pussy after and spit our flavor into your mouth."

Atiana's pussy clenched, her breaths labored as she forgot everything in the world but the man beneath her and the words he was growling at her.

"I can't wait to fill that pussy with my cum. To breed you. To breed my pussy." His thumb played with her clit. "This is my pussy. Yes, baby. Milk me. Fuck, come all over my cock." He clenched his jaw. "Yes, yes, yes..."

CHAPTER 17

EDMUND

As King, Edmund normally wasn't lucky enough to sleuth through the corridors undetected. On occasion, though, especially when the help were too preoccupied with their conversations, he was given the opportunity.

Unfortunately, as Edmund made his way around servants who didn't notice his presence, he was bothered to find the topic was about the one thing he'd been trying to avoid all along. Then, he became disgusted at the words that were spoken about her.

Atiana, the gold digger.

Atiana, the whore.

Atiana, the power-hungry enchantress.

Atiana, the depraved.

The woman who just last week only had nice things said about her. Before, every topic that regarded the tailor was about how lovely she was and how, though quiet about her own life, she was always great with advice, and how much everyone thought her the most pleasant to be around. Women never spoke harshly of her because though she was known to be the most beautiful woman at the palace, she never flaunted it or attempted to gain more attention. If anything, women respected her more for it.

And now, in only two days, all of that had been stripped from her.

Because of him.

They'd known she was friends with the women of the Posse before, but he suspected no one had anticipated how close she'd truly become with them. Likely they thought her only joining the women in their suites in order to fit them for more clothes. Now they spoke of how she'd wedged her way in so that the Posse was made as much a victim to her temptings as he was.

How everyone already knew was beyond him. She'd shown up to his suite two nights prior then spent yesterday with the Posse.

Then he remembered that though dinner had already been placed in the dining hall with the others of the Posse before they'd shown up, a couple servants who'd been bathed in shadows likely would've seen King Edmund walking hand-in-hand with the tailors assistant to be the final ones to show for dinner.

How could he have been so stupid? He hadn't thought much of it. He'd been so sated from their afternoon orgasms, and the corridors had been so clear, that Edmund hadn't thought to be extra cautious. He should've figured out a way to slowly bring her out.

There was no avoiding it now though. Rumors had spread. Rumors accusing Atiana of playing the long game for her own gain. And though part of that statement was true—she had played the long game, though she'd believed to be in an unrequited situation—the second part was entirely false. Atiana was as lovely as everyone had believed her to be. The woman was willing to do anything for them. Edmund was being selfish in allowing it. It was all for his gain, not hers.

"I heard that the reason she kept denying the head tailor position was to make it look inconspicuous when she ditched that wing and took residence in the Queen's wing," one servant muttered to her three friends.

That was preposterous. Atiana denied the position because she hadn't cared for that responsibility, though now if their relationship continued, she'd have a responsibility that far outweighed any other in the palace.

"I heard she's been slowly working through the Queen's wing for years in order to have it just the way she wanted when she decided to strike," another muttered.

Edmund scowled, walking away from them. He wouldn't make himself known and defend her because that would only make the rumors worse. He couldn't fathom how much he'd hear of love potions she'd had smuggled from the Island.

"She needs to spread her legs. Without a child, she won't be guaranteed anything. At least then she'd get the Queen's wing until she dies like the last one." He passed by another gossiping group. Apparently Atiana was the only topic of conversation for the day.

He hated any rumors about her but especially all of the ones he was hearing about the Queen's wing. He couldn't fathom her being farther than two feet from him when they went to bed. The thought of her in another wing entirely made his stomach roil.

Though maybe it shouldn't. Maybe he should consider the repercussions.

If she remained in the tailor's wing, which was far enough away from the King's wing though not as far as the Queen's, then she would be...

Talked about even worse.

Edmund froze as he realized the situation in its entirety for the first time. Everyone knew of them already. There was no more hiding it to protect her. It was either marry her and allow the narrative that she'd connived a long game for that position or leave her and listen to rumors that she was simply his whore or of her failed attempts. Though Edmund wanted to protect her, he realized now that marriage was the only way left to do that.

His heart leapt at the thought. He hated that she would be hurt in any way because of him, but he couldn't help the excitement that now there were no more excuses he could feed himself on why they could not be together.

His heart sped at the possibility of making her his wife.

Then dropped at the thought of her in the Queen's wing.

Then somersaulted when he realized he was going to get rid of that wing entirely, especially now that the Posse was growing so much. It would be time to change up the palace. A fresh start for all the other changes he was going to be making to the North.

Then his heart dropped again because now rumors of all of this being Atiana's doing would spread and there wasn't a thing he could do about it. Those who didn't want to accept magicians would blame her. Those who didn't want to move wings and suites and rooms would blame her. Those who didn't want to begin talks with the Island would blame her.

Then again, as Queen, she would be blamed for far more as the years passed. As King, Edmund was blamed for just about everything.

And there was also the flip side of the coin. Those who loved magicians would credit her. Those who loved the idea of a fresh start with the palace. Those who'd long wanted to communicate and possibly open travel to the Island. They would all credit her.

As Edmund continued his walk, his heart galloped as the angel and devil on either of his shoulders warred.

THE DEVIL WON. Of course it did. The devil almost always won. Especially when it came to protecting his woman.

This time the devil made him realize those two situations hadn't been his only options. There was also number three— they were holding hands because they were about to get into a huge argument with the Posse and he needed to make sure she didn't run. With a little more thought, he could easily flesh out a convincing statement that he would allow servants to over- hear and spread and love for the tailor would once again blossom around the palace. She would be the victim stuck in the Posse's drama.

The angel on his other shoulder cried for the wife he was losing. Edmund himself barely kept the tears from shining in his eyes. Instead he held the dark look Atiana had once thought meant he hated her. Now she knew it was only a way to control himself.

He didn't care if she knew though. She was already aware that he loved her, and he wanted her to know it. He never wished to take those words back, but he couldn't relinquish her to a life of scrutiny. He certainly wasn't worth it.

She was in only one of his white shirts sweeping up the ashes that had fallen to the ground before the fireplace when he walked into his suite. It was such a domestic sight. Never in his past marriage had Rowena done anything like that. She'd been the epitome of what people expected of a Queen, sitting about as if she was too good to do any work herself. With how power-hungry that woman had been, it wasn't surprising.

Atiana, on the other hand, cleaned his suite and wore his shirts and mended her own things. She was the very idea of a wife. A real one.

Edmund's heart tore in half, the angel begging him to just marry her.

The devil was louder. Much louder. And that fucker loved to see Edmund suffer.

"You shouldn't be here," he opened.

She gave a cheeky smile as she brushed the ashes to a corner to be picked up later. "Oh yeah? And where do I have to be that is more important? I can work on the blankets and garments for the other towns from here." She nodded toward the corner of the common space where a chair was set up with thread and needle.

"People will wonder where you are when they cannot find you in your suite. You should go back."

She finally leaned the broom against the wall and turned to him, her smile diminishing as she took in the darkness of his eyes. "What is it now? What new argument will you give now?"

"There is no new argument, Atiana. There are already rumors. Sick, vile rumors. You need to leave before they get worse."

She scoffed. "Don't you think they'll be even worse then? I'd be your *whore*, Edmund."

He shook his head. "The boys and I have lied about far worse to the rest of the palace. We will come up with the excuse for why we were seen together and have that spread by midday tomorrow."

She gave an unamused laugh. "And if I don't agree?"

"I don't remember giving you a choice."

She narrowed her gorgeous eyes as her hands folded over her chest making the white shirt rise on her thighs. Tempting. Far too tempting. "No? How do you expect to get me out of here then?"

"I'll make sure no one is around the King's wing. You can surely make it back to the tailor's wing without notice."

"Oh yes. Surely *I* can." She quirked a brow. "Too bad I'm not leaving."

"Atiana!" He stepped forward knowing he was larger and more terrifying as he took up more space. With the flames in the fireplace lighting him, he probably looked damn near the devil on his shoulder. "You are leaving. Now!"

"Are you taking me? Because unless you throw me over your shoulder, I'm not going anywhere. And if you do that, you'll attract far more attention."

"Why are you being difficult?"

"Why are you being an idiot?"

He took a large breath in. "I'm trying to protect you."

"*I'm* trying not to murder *you*."

He almost laughed. His good little Northern girl never spoke in such a manner. It was sexy. If her safety—more emotional and mental than physical—wasn't on the line, he'd grab her face and kiss the fuck out of her.

He had to figure out what to do. He loved this woman more than life itself. How did his men do this? How did Sparrow and Miels, Killian and James and Tristan handle their feelings for their women?

He took a very deep breath in. "I'm not going to marry you."

Pain like he'd never felt rushed through him. Every single tip of his body felt it. His knees grew weak and his head rushed with an ache, his fingers became clammy and his chest sore.

He wanted to shield her.

And instead, he'd just caused the worst edge of hurt to line her beautiful eyes. That sassy woman who had just been arguing with him was gone and in its place was a broken one.

He'd done this to her. Not the rumors or the others within the palace, but him. With only a single statement.

"Then I really am your whore, huh?" The words left her in the softest, saddest whisper.

"Atiana—" He stepped for her.

She stepped back.

The angel clawed in his chest to take her in his arms and promise they'd be married as soon as Tristan was back at the palace, but the devil was strong. It sat on his shoulders and controlled him.

"I'll meet with the others to figure out the lie we'll pass." He turned without a second glance and left the suite, needing to be away from her before he hurt her anymore.

CHAPTER 18
ATIANA

To think that a man as intellectual and strategic as him could be the biggest idiot to grace the lands was unimaginable.

She was hurt. Of course she was. Even knowing he'd only said it to make her hate him like before, she couldn't fight how well it worked. He wanted to marry her. He'd spent all the night before whispering to her about how he couldn't wait for Tristan to be back so he could make her his wife already. She'd fallen asleep to those beautiful words. The ones he'd just spoken were the lie.

But they still bloody hurt.

I'm not going to marry you.

She hadn't believed it, but the pain of how prepared he'd been to use that against her—the possibility of making her his actual whore—was too much to bear. She'd needed time alone and had been glad he'd been the one to turn around. She'd been serious about not leaving the suite, but she'd needed time away from him.

It hadn't even been an hour. Maybe all of thirty minutes

had passed before she was pacing the common space, antsy for him to come back already. But maybe his absence was good. She was so annoyed with him and needed time to think of how to convince him she was ready for all the rumors as long as she had him.

After another hour, Atiana decided her best course of action was to compare her willingness to take on the scrutiny to his willingness to let go of her. They were both doing it out of love, except at the end of hers, they would both be happy. At the end of his, they'd be miserable. Hopefully the big oaf wasn't single-minded enough to finally *hear* her.

With her mind made up, Atiana was tired of pacing the suite. She simply wanted him to come back.

Huffing, she turned back to the pile of ashes she'd left by the fireplace and cleaned it into the dustpan choosing to throw it into the bin in Edmund's office before dragging said bin toward the door to remind herself to throw the bag out later.

Edmund's office was through a door directly across from the entrance to the King's suite and an even broodier room than the rest of his suite. Before the events of an hour prior, he'd informed her she was allowed to change any part of the suite, make it as bright as she liked, except for his office. Atiana hadn't been sure when he mentioned it. His suite was so moody, but it was also him. And given it was a space for them to relax together, she'd felt comfortable leaving it as is. She might change her mind in a few years but for now, the suite was perfect.

This office was beautiful.

An accented rug blended perfectly with the mahogany and leather furniture and the curtains were thick and mostly closed to keep much of the day away. Most of the walls held smaller frames of past relatives or achievements, but for one corner. Sitting on the ground with a sheet over the top half was a large painting. In it were Evony and Rosaelia, the former's eyes a dead giveaway for what she was. Both girls were giggly and beautiful, and Atiana pictured her own children looking just like them as babies.

Atiana took a moment standing by the door to contemplate her next move before she did it. Edmund wouldn't care. As ludicrous as he was being at the moment, she knew he wanted her to know all of him. And she was a past part of him.

She slowly moved for the painting and shuffled the sheet out of the way to reveal the late Queen of the Northern Lands. Rowena had been a beautiful woman, and Atiana picked up on similarities they both shared. Both she and that woman had dark brown hair and lighter brown eyes, and Atiana knew the woman had been a bit taller than the average like she was. It was clear the King had a type even if he hadn't loved his late wife.

Staring at the woman who would've been a couple years younger than Atiana was at the moment when she'd gotten this painting commissioned, Atiana was surprised she didn't find any twinge of jealousy arise within her. Even with the woman long dead and gone, she was the mother of his daughters. Atiana had expected uncertainty to come up, especially given how similar they were.

But it wasn't there.

Edmund loved her. He'd never loved his late wife. He wasn't the same person he'd been when he'd married all those years ago.

Her lips twitched up as she met the woman's gaze in the painting. "He hates you for what you tried to do to his daughters, but I think he will always be grateful to you. Both because you had both of his daughters, but also because it was you who kept the second safe from his hand. I know I'll always be grateful. They're no daughters to me, but they are great friends. And

Rosaelia was the catalyst to his change. He learned to love with her, and I will always be grateful to you for creating *that* man."

At peace, Atiana found the two chunky babies once more, one with emerald eyes and the other with sapphire. She wondered as she took in their complexions and black hair if her own children would inherit so completely from their father. She hoped at least one did.

Placing the sheet back in its place covering the late Queen, Atiana left the room.

The main space was still silent except for the roaring fire.

Atiana sighed as she turned to the right for the double doors across from what led to Edmund's—theirs because she would not allow him to destroy what they had—bedroom.

The space was mostly empty with a few pieces of furniture within it. Edmund had mentioned turning it into a room for her to work out of, but Atiana had instantly had other ideas.

Now she smiled widely knowing what babies that came from Edmund looked like.

In her imaginings, they had three to four in boy-girl order, so Atiana leaned against the wall and pictured turning this into a baby boy's nursery. It was large enough for two children to share, but she settled on the first alone. Atiana had always been about enjoying each moment, so she slowed her dreams and settled on the way she would wobble into this room after birth with a tiny newborn in her arms as her husband put the finishing touches to the room together. The babe would sleep by their side for the first bit of his life, but Atiana still smiled as she pictured it.

Edmund loved moody rooms, but she imagined this one painted a pastel blue with a nature hewn wallpaper to bring light to their babe's world, and to represent both of his sisters.

She imagined the crib in the middle of the room over a rug that looked exactly like the one Edmund had in his office but in the lightest shades of blues and grays. With a chair in the corner by one of the large windows, she pictured rocking the babe to sleep as the sun shined through the light shades. Atiana already knew Evony and Rosaelia would want to put their own touches to their brother's room, and she was excited to give that to them.

Another huff passed her lips as Atiana came back to the present and saw the room as it currently was. Dark beige walls, deep brown curtains blocking out most of the light, and three velvet seats, one ottoman, and two small tables. There was nothing special about this room, nothing like what she'd been picturing. Not now, and if Edmund continued to push her away, not ever.

Tears clouded Atiana's eyes as she slid down the wall she was leaning against and brought her knees to her chest.

The tears quickly dried, not falling, and Atiana simply breathed.

She didn't want to think of futures anymore. She did so every day for nearly seven years. Futures with Edmund as her husband and their children running circles around them.

Now she wanted to think of the now. The one where she was seated in an empty room in his suite waiting for him to come back and decide whether he was going to ruin their lives or finally start them.

She pictured him in the present. In that very moment. Was he with his Posse or was he trying to be alone? Was he training or was he in an abandoned room? Was he out in the greens working or perhaps in the forests lining the edges of the palace?

Was he thinking about her? About their future? Was he weighing the pros and cons of his decisions compared to hers? She highly doubted it. He was so moronic sometimes, he couldn't see reason. She didn't entirely blame him as being

Prince under an unjust King, then King himself his entire life, the man thought all of his decisions were sound. Sure he had the Posse to remind him of other ways, but she doubted there'd ever been a case where love was the matter. Not before the start of this year when Evony joined them in the palace that is.

Atiana. A voice sounded in her head, making Atiana jump and stare around right as it stated, *It's Evony. Mind magic.*

It took a moment for the bout of fear to disappear before Atiana felt that she could respond, *Hi. This is definitely a different way to talk.*

Why do you sound so sad? She immediately said back.

You can tell I sound sad through my thoughts?

Because she knew Evony so well, Atiana was sure the girl was smirking as she responded with, *I've been speaking through minds my whole life. I can pick up things like any other conversation.*

Fascinating.

Don't try to divert. What's wrong?

Atiana sighed. She shouldn't tell her anything about her father, but as she slumped against the wall to that room she now knew would be a beautiful nursery, she realized that maybe his daughters would be just the help she required.

Are you able to bring Rosaelia in too?

CHAPTER 19

EDMUND

His back ached from having spent the night sleeping on the stacks on the edge of the private training room, but he'd had to stay away from his suite. Even with her gone, her scent would be everywhere.

"Damn it," Sparrow cursed as steps lured Edmund to turn for the door that led to the palace.

Miels was smirking, and Edmund knew he'd just won a bet. "I told you he'd be here. Where else would he have to go?"

"What the bloody hell do you want?" he muttered as he lifted himself to sit up and found not only the two boys but all the members of the Posse who were currently at the palace.

"How many more times are you going to try to push Atiana away?" Rosaelia asked instead.

Edmund groaned. The very last thing he needed was his daughters angry with him. "How do you know about that?"

"Women speak, father," she sniped.

It was so rare an occasion for his first daughter to be mad at him that it immediately caught his attention and made him sit up, sighing. "She came to you."

"No…" Both daughters looked sheepish then, not meeting his gaze, and fuck, did they look like they'd grown up getting into trouble together.

Edmund narrowed his gaze at the two before they snapped to Evony. "How many times have I told you to stay out of our heads?"

She rolled her eyes, meeting his eyes once more. "To be fair, I wasn't snooping. I went into her head to ask her to join us, but we were all the way at the other end of the palace, and I was tired, so I didn't want to go get her. She was upset. *She* asked me to link in Ro."

"*She* did?"

Evony shrugged. "I guess she wanted both of your daughters to know you're an idiot. Again, her words."

Edmund shook his head. "And everyone else just happened to hear your mind conversation?"

Evony smirked. "Etel was with us. It'd be rude to not add her. And we all know we tell our men everything. And Gemma and I are basically sisters, so she had to know, and she also tells her man everything."

"Though I regret not having been able to raise you, I cannot imagine the troublemaker you would've been as a child."

She giggled. "Thank you."

Rosaelia snagged his attention once more. "Really, Father? You'd rather we come up with a lie than own your relationship? I understand where your heart is at, trust me, but you're hurting her far more than any whispers ever could. And you're not doing it with an end in sight. At least when I left Kill to go after that woman"—she hadn't been able to say Mom since finding out about Rowena, and though Edmund was happy about it, a part of him hurt for her—"I knew I intended on going back and making things right. You're leaving her to suffer."

Etel was tentative as she moved from her husband's side and took a seat beside Edmund on the stacks. She didn't entirely meet his gaze, and her voice was soft as she said, "I get your worries."

Silence followed her statement.

And Edmund swore he felt a bit of fear. That having one person on his side would make him stick firm to his decisions.

"I... I stayed away from Miels because I was worried about the rumors too. We were together in secret the way you and Atiana have been. He wanted to show me off, to have me move in. I didn't allow it. I couldn't fathom the amount of hatred that would come my way. I couldn't live with the thought that everyone would believe I got to where I am because I was... spreading my legs for Miels." She said the last bit in almost a whisper, her cheeks turning pink.

"Thank you. I cannot put her through that much pain."

Etel nodded, finally looking up. "It did hurt. A lot of people had things to say. Never to my face of course because they were afraid of what the Posse might do, but rumors did spread. But... not as much as you'd expect." Her lips tipped to a close-lipped smile at his furrowed brows. "Some, surely. But... everyone knew me already. They knew of my talents. They still respected them. The same way everyone knows of Atiana's talents, respects hers.

"Plus, it's really only truly bad the first week or two. When the shock is the largest. After the first week, when a bit of that envy—which is entirely reasonable—subsides, most people remember the person before the Posse. And when I still acted the same as before, if anything, becoming more fun, our relationship became so normal, I had people commenting that it felt like we'd been together for years rather than weeks.

"So, yes, I understand your fear, but... I also know what it's like to be on the other side. And so does Atiana." She smiled to herself. "When I was fighting myself about Miels, Atiana told me she loved someone and she would go through any gossip to be with him. She's a lot stronger than you're giving her credit for, Ed. She'll be able to handle it."

Edmund focused back on the group and found such pride in Miels's face. That was the same look Edmund always had to hide when Atiana did something amazing. He couldn't fathom how exciting it might feel to allow others to see it.

Edmund finally met his daughters' gazes, Rosaelia's in particular. "You two would truly be okay with her? She is closer to your age than mine." He must've really needed reassurance that he wouldn't be ruining his woman's life because not an ounce of him had thought to ask his daughters whether they were okay with the relationship before bringing Atiana to dinner the other night.

Rosaelia shrugged. "She might be my best friend. And you're my best friend. Of course I would like the two of you together."

Edmund shook his head. "I'm too old. She needs someone who could give her a life. With kids and—"

"She told us you keep talking about getting her pregnant," Evony interrupted.

Edmund's eyebrows shot up. "She did?"

Evony smirked. "We're very close."

"Why are you okay with that? Why are any of you okay with that? I'm about to be a grandfather. I cannot be a father again!"

"Oh, come now, King," Evony started. "Do not act so bewildered. The two of you have thirsted for one another for so long, you know you want to still be in that room. Holed up and inside her. We all know it. Did you really expect us to believe you're going to keep coming in her without babies? With the way you love her? You're going to want versions of the two of you like our men do. So, no, we don't care that you want to come in her until you breed her."

Edmund narrowed his eyes at the Magician. "You seem to forget I'm your father."

She smirked. "You seem to forget that is not how I grew up. To me, you are more a friend. One whom I will tease to my heart's content."

Edmund's narrowed gaze turned up to her husband. "I see you haven't learned how to control your wife."

Sparrow smirked. "I can control my wife perfectly well, Ed. I simply choose my battles, and this is not one I feel the need to stop."

Rosaelia was bright pink, but she cleared her throat for her father's attention anyway. "I wouldn't have put it as crassly or bluntly as my dear twin, but... what she said was true. I would love for Atiana to have your babies. I know you would love it more than anything in the world."

"You cannot allow Rowena to control you anymore," Sparrow stated in the silence after.

"Excuse me?"

"She's made you question everything after this past year. You're allowing her to control your actions."

"What's that to mean?"

"Before this year, had you known Atiana wanted you, you would have taken on whatever hurt," Miels answered. "Now, you're closing up."

"She fucked with your head. She knew how you would react, and you still feel guilt for Evony," James stated, and Edmund realized this was a conversation they'd had because James hadn't known him before.

"And you feel guilty for Sael," Killian finally spoke.

"Because she almost killed the daughter you'd raised. As if any of that was your fault."

Rosaelia held out her hand and patiently waited. After a moment of silence, Edmund stood from the stacks and reached for her.

"She made you think too much about everything but your heart. You've always been strategic about relationships, but you never let that cross into your personal ones. Now you're allowing it to control you. Your heart knows you wish for Atiana. But because of that woman, you're afraid of the outcomes. You're strategizing rather than living, and we don't do that in our personal relationships, Father. You need to *live*."

Staring into her perfect emerald eyes, Edmund realized that maybe they were right. He internally scoffed to himself. Of course they were right. Long gone and forever dead now, but Rowena still had this control over the way he perceived relationships. And not only in the way they'd stated but also with the fears of another Queen like her. As if his Atiana was anything like that monster. As if she hungered for power or was too weak to take the snide remarks Rowena had always made a problem over.

Atiana was... unafraid.

So very unlike him it would seem, for he was scared for her. The very last thing he wanted was for her to suffer, but Edmund hadn't stopped to think about the actual future. One where they had to pretend that nothing had happened between them, where they had to stay away from one another even though neither of them would stop loving the other. He'd been so focused on the present, that picturing the future now seemed... unbearable. Even with the rumors that followed them, he couldn't fathom any future where not being together would cause less suffering than the alternative.

Shocked by his own stupidity, Edmund gave his daughter a

small smile and leaned in to kiss her crow. "Thank you." She squeezed his hands as he kissed her once more, then turned to kiss Evony's crown as well, ignoring everyone's grins and knowing gazes as he marched out of the private training room for her suite by the tailor's wing. He didn't hide his intentions as others, servants of all decrees, passed him by. He didn't care what they believed, didn't care that more than a few of them stopped to watch his back as he turned for Atiana's door and banged on it.

Nothing happened.

"Atiana, open the door."

Even if they hadn't been watching or hypothesizing, they would be now. And he didn't care. He wouldn't keep his voice down. There were to be rumors, that was a fact. Edmund was now done worrying about them and focused on his future.

But as he banged on the door, nothing.

"Atiana!"

Nothing.

He heard shuffling behind him but did not care to turn for which servants they were. If she was determined that she did not mind all the talk that would come of their relationship, then he would allow for it to properly become known.

"Atiana, my love. Please open the door." He banged again.

Still nothing. Not even a sound from within.

Edmund grumbled and tried the knob to find it unlocked. When he stepped within, it was silent. Empty.

He quickly tried the small bedroom off to the side of this common space to find it equally barren.

Edmund's brows furrowed. "Atiana," he called, not expecting an answer.

She wasn't there.

His heart raced. Had he gone too far? Had she picked up all her things and left him? She'd mentioned before that she could not bear a life without him. Had he finally pushed her over the edge? He would not be able to live with himself if that were the case. He would not be able to rule as King without his Queen. He would abandon all else to find her.

Edmund swiveled to her chest of drawers to ease the panic building within him. It did not help. The drawers were empty.

He turned then to the armoire. It, too, was swiped clean.

"Atiana," he called to the void, racing back to the small common space to notice now that her sewing material was also gone. "No. No, no, no! Atiana!"

He would not endure a life without her.

Edmund reached for the piece of cloth he always carried to calm himself down enough to think and did not find it where it normally rested in his pocket. His panic exploded then as if this was an omen to her disappearance.

Edmund swiveled quickly, moving for his rooms and ignoring everyone pushed against the walls watching him. Let them see how deeply he'd gone for her, let them see the greatest weakness to their King. Because she was also his greatest strength.

And he needed to find her.

He needed to find that damned cloth to help calm himself down, then run off after her, wherever she'd gone.

When Edmund finally, mercifully, burst into his suite on the brink of tears, he stopped abruptly. Sitting on his couch by the roaring fire, ashes once again dusting the ground around her, with her feet tucked under some pillows and a small book in her hands, was the woman his entire world revolved around.

"Atiana," he croaked, relief flooding in faster than he could take it.

She looked at him with wide eyes, dropping the book and rushing to his side. "Edmund? Edmund, what's happened?"

When her hands landed on his face and chest to check him

over for injury, Edmund finally allowed that final breath of relief as he released the door to shut behind him. "You're here."

"Of course I'm here. Where else would I be? Now tell me, what's happened?"

He shook his head, reveling in her hands scattering across his body. "You weren't in your suite."

"Because I've been here."

"Your things weren't there."

"Because they're here."

"Here?" he said numbly.

She squared her shoulders as if waiting for another argument but there was determination in her eyes. "Here."

He laughed, nearly hysterical, as he pulled her into him, holding on for dear life. "Thank the fucking lords, my love."

Her hands were tentative as they reached around his form, unsure whether to hold on or push him away. "Are you going to tell me what happened?"

He pulled back only enough to look her in the eyes. "I've been a fucking idiot."

She stared at him with a quirked brow. "Are you expecting me to deny it? You have."

He chuckled, cradling her face and bringing her in close. "No. Don't deny it. Put me in my place, love. Lords know you're the only one I'd allow to speak to me in such manners."

Her fingers gripped the front of his shirt as hope burst into her eyes. "In private?"

He smirked. "Considering the scene I just made in your rooms when I thought you'd run away from me, I don't think any lie we try to come up with will be convincing or that anything about us will remain a secret. And especially not once there's a wedding to organize."

She clutched on tighter to him. "A wedding?"

His thumb brushed her bottom lip. "I told you at the beginning, Atiana. I want to breed you. But I want you to be my wife first."

"Truly?"

"Would you like me to drop to my knees and beg?"

Mischief lit in her eyes as she smirked, such an uncommon look on her beautiful features. "I wouldn't mind it."

Edmund dropped immediately, and she gasped, obviously not expecting him to do it so suddenly. "I will beg for eternity, my love. I'll place you on the throne and beg you in front of every lord and stationed noble in the lands. I will take you to each village and beg you in front of every common folk."

Atiana giggled, and it was the most stunning of sounds. Then she dropped to her knees before him and cradled his face gently. "No need for all that, my King."

"Then you will marry me? Become my wife?"

"I was beginning to think I would need to demand it of you."

He chuckled. "Maybe I should take it back and allow you to."

She grinned, that mischief still twinkling in her eyes, as she brought him in close. "You will marry me, my King."

"Love," he corrected. "Your love."

She bit her bottom lip, and Edmund instantly became jealous. "You will marry me, my love."

"As you wish, *my Queen*."

She kissed him softly, and he took over with all the passion he was feeling. Then pulled away abruptly.

Before she could complain, he held her face in his hands. "That was fun." Her furrowed brows were entirely too adorable. "But let's do this right." He took her hands into his and met her eyes softly. "Atiana St. Bonémore. Will you do me the honor of gifting me your presence for the rest of our lives?

Will you rule this kingdom by my side as Queen and my heart as Goddess? Will you marry me?"

Her fingers wiggled in his hands like she couldn't contain herself. "Eternally, my love."

This time, Edmund didn't stop himself from leaning over and kissing her with everything he had.

EPILOGUE

EDMUND

Her body was so pliant, so responsive. Anything he did to her, her body fell into place. Every touch caused a moan so endearing he nearly came from the sound alone.

And she was absolutely breathtaking against the windows of his private shower. Daybreak was just on the horizon, and given it was now winter, there was no longer a bush of greens outside his window nor the cover he used in the winter months to block outdoor sight, so Edmund knew though not many people would be outside to see them at this hour from his ground-floor rooms, they very well could. And at that moment, he didn't care if they all saw. Atiana was his. Let everyone at the palace know not to touch her lest they wish to end their lives.

His Northern blood pushed the notion of being watched aside as his hands slithered up Atiana's wet thighs, the water pounding down his back. As lovely as the bathtub to the side had seemed, he was especially glad they'd chosen a "quick" shower instead. Her head was thrown back, hands scratching at the window for something to hold on to as Edmund suckled at the side of her neck, his fingers inching over her round behind until they breached that puckered hole.

Atiana gasped and her hips thrust into him, her cunt sliding against his straining hard cock. "Edmund, please."

He chuckled at her ear. "I thought I wasn't allowed anywhere near your butt, my love."

Her head shook frantically. "You're allowed everywhere. Every hole is yours. Please fill it."

Edmund chuckled again as his fingertips grazed the edge of her ass while his mouth switched sides to leave his mark on the right side of her neck as well. "Which one, my love? Which hole would you like filled?"

"All of them!" she exclaimed as her hips became frantic, rubbing against him. She was taking herself to orgasm, and Edmund delighted in being used this way.

With her legs wrapped around his waist, Atiana writhed against his cock until she was shaking with orgasm, crying out his name.

Edmund smirked as he lifted her into his arms and carried her to the edge of their bed, falling over her. "You're sopping wet for me, my love."

Her eyes were glossed over with lust as she met his gaze from beneath long lashes. "We need to be getting down. People will be expecting us soon."

Edmund chuckled. "People can kiss my ass. I'm not leaving this room until I've had my fill, and I'm certainly not leaving before I've satisfied my wife. Now, what was it you wanted? Oh yes, to fill all your holes."

She swallowed but that small smile told him she was still excited to be completely filled.

His thumb rubbed her kiss-swollen lips. "Don't be nervous,

sweetheart. My cock won't be making it's way into your ass today. I'll ease my way there."

"You're so crass." Her lips lifted a little more.

He bit her jaw with a growl. "Only for you." Then before she could say anything more, he flipped her onto her stomach, and lifted her hips so her ass was propped up enough to drop a pillow beneath.

His hands slithered over her back until her was at her ass, caressing each cheek before giving one, then the other, a smack hard enough to leave his mark. He soothed the pain with light caresses again as he enjoyed the way she mewled beneath him.

Propped on his knees, he kneaded at her ass some more before spreading her cheeks and spitting into the middle. Atiana yelped with the feel before a moan left her.

Edmund sent his thumb through her cunt to soak in her arousal before coming back up to tease her puckered hole. "Such a pretty, pretty view, my love."

Atiana moaned, clenching at the unfamiliar touch, but did not move away from him.

"That's my good girl. Let me in," he prompted as he slowly moved his thumb inside her. He pumped the tip in a few times to get her comfortable before going any deeper. "How does that feel, baby?"

Her moans were unintelligible but the way she thrust her ass up at him reassured him that she was greedy for more.

Edmund enjoyed the sight of his thumb getting lost in the most divine ass he'd ever laid eyes upon, licking his lips as he imagined all the things he'd do to her in the future.

"More, please! More!" she begged, making Edmund smirk.

"My greedy, greedy whore." Edmund smacked her ass with his free hand as he lined his cock up to her cunt and thrust in hard, his thumb never breaking pace in her ass. "Fuck!" He smacked her ass again. "Fuck, you're so sexy with my hand-prints marking you."

"Yes, yes, yes." She gripped the sheets and thrust back into him.

Edmund chuckled as he fucked her hard, but his gaze darkened on the back of her head. "You like that, my whore?"

"Mhmmm."

"But I haven't filled all your holes yet."

She moaned, yelled really. "Please!"

Edmund fucked her ass harder, matching pace with his thrusts as he gripped the back of her hair and snapped her head back. "Give me that mouth."

She reached back for him immediately like his obedient little whore.

He bit at her mouth. "That's my fucking girl." His tongue was harsh as he kissed her, ravished her.

She was coming but he held her in place, wanting control over her body even as it lost all of it to pleasure.

He kissed her harder, eating her up, wanting to thrust himself deeper and harder into every one of her holes. "Fuuckk." He bit her bottom lip as his eyes rolled back. "You're ruining me."

"Good," she barely breathed as her hips thrashed back harder.

Then he was kissing her again, dominating her body with his cock and hands while he commanded her breaths with his harsh tongue. She belonged to him, and fuck, did he enjoy reminding himself.

When she came a second time, moans hidden in his mouth, her cunt clenched onto his cock so tightly, he couldn't hold back from coming inside her, filling her until his cum was seeping out and onto her thighs.

Only when his cock lost all will to stay fully hard did

Edmund pull away slowly, dropping first her head to the bed so she was lying face down, then his thumb from her ass. His cock was the last to leave her, and only after he thrust into her a final time.

Enjoying the sight of her ravished beneath him, Edmund took the cum on her thighs and forced it back inside her pussy.

She moaned and her cunt clenched, and Edmund grinned as he leaned down to bite her asscheek.

When he rose back to his knees, he licked his lips taking in the view before grabbing both sides of her hips and flipping her to her back. He removed the pillow she'd been propped on and slithered up her body.

Edmund kissed her stomach softly. "I cannot wait to watch you grow large with my child."

She wore a soft smile, exhausted but content. "You've done it before."

Edmund didn't look up, so transfixed with her belly as he was. "We were a contractual marriage. Rowena and I married simply because I needed an heir. We had sex for said heir, and she spent all of her time in her wing and I in mine. It was nothing like this. I would never allow us separate win—"

"I don't want a separate wing," Atiana interrupted.

Edmund kissed her belly. "Because we are a love match. I will be here for every part of your pregnancy, my love. I will be here to kiss your belly as it grows swollen, to speak to our babe as he grows, to help you in any way you need, be it massages or simply holding you."

Atiana's eyes had tears lining them when he finally looked up.

"Did I say something wrong?"

She smiled. "Never. I simply cannot wait to carry your children."

He smirked. "Children? We're having more than one?"

"Given your daughters, we could have twins."

He shrugged. "I believe that was from their mother's side."

Her hand fell into his hair. "Do you not want multiple?"

He scoffed, kissing her belly again. "Do not go based on what I want, my love. If it were up to me, you'd remain pregnant for the next decade."

She gasped. "That's at least nine children."

He smirked up at her. "Told you. Don't go off of what I want."

The fire crackling was the only sound for a while before Atiana said, "I think I want four. Maybe five. Though who knows. The more time I spend with you, the higher that number gets."

Edmund sighed a breath of relief as his forehead fell to her stomach. "Thank the lords."

Atiana giggled. "You're quite ridiculous, Your Highness."

Edmund bit her stomach before traveling up her body until their lips brushed. "Ridiculous, my love? For wanting to breed you?"

"For being relieved about having seven children."

His brows lifted with a teasing, "You want seven now?"

"I was including your daughters."

He bit her bottom lip. "I love you, Atiana. I want everything with you."

Atiana kissed him slowly as her legs slithered open. "I love you too, Edmund."

"Good." His tongue ravished her mouth as his cock, now fully erect again, slithered down her slit, then sank deep into her as he swallowed their moans. "Because we're not leaving this suite until you're carrying my child."

ALLURING DARKNESS

NELLY ALIKYAN

ALLURING DARKNESS
PROLOGUE

Vera kept her gaze facing forward and forced her eyes to remain dry. She would not cry over something so pathetic.

The job she'd just lost was quite pathetic, but more so than anything else was that she hadn't been able to hold a job down for over a year now. Losing her father had affected her more than she cared to admit.

On top of all that, Vera knew she didn't want to do any of the jobs she continued to get. She wanted, more than anything, to begin a freelance baking business for herself. To be able to bake and bake and make money from it. Nothing sounded better. But nothing sounded more expensive either. What with starting, building clientele, and everything that went into running a small business. That brought tears back to Vera's eyes.

No, she wouldn't cry.

She would hold herself up and do what she always did—look for another job.

Resolved with her decision, Vera was determined to make

it home as soon as she could and begin the search for this new job. Plus, she was about a week away from getting kicked out of her apartment, so there was no choice but to make something work, it was all she had left.

Vera was walking down Main Street on the way back to her place when the tugging feeling deep in her core began. It was the same uncomfortableness she always felt around this part of town, but apparently no one else had the same sensation. When Vera had asked others if they felt it too, they had looked at her oddly. So no, they didn't feel anything. Vera was alone in that too.

The tugging, which felt like a string was attached to the inside of her lower belly and was pulling upwards, began when she walked toward the end of Main Street. It had started not long after her father passed away, but it always seemed to ebb away, so Vera never put too much thought into it.

But the tugging wasn't going away. It was getting stronger.

"Great," Vera thought aloud as she placed her hand to her stomach as if it were merely a cramp. "Just what I needed today."

She moved her gaze to the shop fronts as she continued walking and realized why the tugging hadn't gone away; she'd never walked in this direction. Normally she took the alleyway between the cafe and the boutique to walk back to her place, but it seemed today, Vera had chosen a different path.

The tugging feeling tightened and now was beginning to feel a bit more like a cramp, but she'd never felt a cramp like this before.

Trying to ignore it and hoping it would go away soon, Vera neared the next alleyway she knew would lead back to her place. She needed to find a job and an apartment to keep.

Passing the eyewear store, Vera came closer to the corner

that lead to the alley she needed, Vera felt the tugging shoot straight through her and bent forward, no longer able to hold herself up. She grasped her knees and held tight as she tried to breathe the pain away.

She looked up to see herself mirrored in the dusty shop window. Her brown spiral curls were seated by her shoulders, just as they always were, the fronts held back by a clip. Though a couple of curls fell forward, Vera saw past the hair to the deep brown eyes staring back at her. Her face was scrunched, and Vera knew she did not want anyone to find her in this position. She wouldn't be able to hide the humiliation.

Allowing her gaze to move a bit higher, Vera noticed she'd stopped in front of an old antique shop she'd never seen before.

Slowly picking herself back to a standing position, she glanced around and breathed a sigh of relief that no one had been around to see her. She looked back to the shop and felt the tugging in her core was now pulling her forward as if begging to enter the store.

"So this is what the tugging is about," Vera whispered to herself but didn't know what to think about the whole thing.

Testing her walking, she found that her body was adjusting to the sensation in her abs, so she stepped into the antique shop.

Impossibly, the tugging seemed to grow stronger, but the pain wasn't there. Instead, it felt like a persistent child trying to pull their mom to the toy they wanted.

Vera strolled into the cluster of the store, finding stacks of old chests, toys, and rocking chairs. Blankets and clothes and mirrors. The store was piled so high and so tight that the walking paths were hardly big enough for one person.

As she followed the tugging, Vera scanned the piles, finding old storybooks, typewriters, and albums. She took in everything around her, but didn't stop for any of it.

Given she wasn't paying attention to the path before her, Vera didn't notice until it was too late that she had bumped into a man. Holding out her arms to steady him, she noticed the man's arms tightened around a storybook he held close to his chest as if he were afraid she would try to steal it from him.

Vera looked up to find an attractive man looking down at her, though fear laced his gaze as he pulled the book closer to his chest. He was bald with a light goatee and glasses. Dorky, but cute.

"I'm sorry," Vera said softly. "I wasn't paying attention."

She ignored the persistent tugging as she watched him. He nodded quickly to her apology and walked past her to the counter. Vera furrowed her brows and again whispered to herself, "Odd. But then again, what part of any of this," she pointed to her stomach, "isn't odd?"

Turning again, she followed the sensation around the store. Passing a pile of books on an old chestnut dresser, Vera felt the tugging hit a crescendo. She braced herself on the dresser and looked down to her stomach. "Okay. I get it."

The feeling eased ever so slightly. Enough for Vera to turn her attention to the pile of books, unsure if that's what was so important.

She grabbed the book on the top of the pile and held it, feeling the tugging pull, as if saying this wasn't it. She placed the book to the side and tried the next one. Again, this wasn't it.

Vera tried book after book until her hands fell onto the second to last in the pile, and the tugging eased completely. That feeling was more odd than not, given Vera had gotten used to the tugging, and she now felt a soreness in her abs as if she'd been doing crunches the past half hour.

Ignoring that, Vera paid attention to the book in her hands. Somehow, this book had caused a tugging sensation to bring her to it.

It looked like an old Wiccan book the witches always had in movies. Bracing it on one arm, Vera flipped through it and glanced at the tons of spells and descriptions and drawings. It was a cool book, but Vera had no idea what this had to do with her.

Coming to the end, Vera was ready to close it when she noticed the edge of a picture. Holding the end of the book open, Vera paused short as paralysis took hold of her body.

Taped to the end of this book was a picture of her mother and father standing in front of an old Victorian house, and in her mother's arms was a baby Vera. It was the exact same picture she had framed in her room.

Vera lightly touched the picture, wondering about her mother and missing her father dearly.

Her mother had left her as a baby, and the part of Vera that should resent her for it couldn't. Her father had never allowed that. He had always made sure her mother was loved in their household.

And her father, her best friend, had passed away over a year ago, and she still felt the pain every single day.

As her eyes began to water, Vera touched her tongue to the base of her mouth to stop the freefall and glanced at the other picture taped right beside her family one. It was another picture of her mother, but this time, she was holding a little girl on either knee. Girls that looked a bit like her mother, a bit like Vera herself.

Gasping, Vera brought the book closer to her face, but couldn't believe what she was seeing. Sisters. She had sisters.

She let go of the breath she'd been holding and slammed the book shut. Holding it to her chest as tightly as the man before had been holding his storybook, Vera walked up to the counter and bought it.

She was now determined to get home, but for an entirely different purpose: she had sisters to find.

Continue the Whittle Magic series in
Alluring Darkness...

DON'T FORGET TO REVIEW!

Thank you so much for finishing your read! Don't forget to leave a review or rating on all platforms as it helps me as an author more than you can ever imagine!

Amazon and Goodreads ratings help the most but feel free to talk about it everywhere else too—including social medias, blogs, Youtube reviews, and most importantly—word of mouth, and more.

FOLLOW NELLY'S SOCIAL MEDIA

Follow Nelly's social media to get the scoop as it's happening!

- tiktok.com/authornellyalikyan
- instagram.com/authornellyalikyan
- youtube.com/NellyAlikyan
- amazon.com/author/nellyalikyan
- goodreads.com/nellyalikyan
- facebook.com/authornellyalikyan
- pinterest.com/insinpublishing

JOIN NELLY'S NEWSLETTER

Sign up for Nelly Alikyan's newsletter to be the first to know about new releases and cover reveals, receive exclusive content —like a special scene or two—and be up to date about any other exciting news, i.e. events, signed copies, etc.

www.nellyalikyan.com

ACKNOWLEDGMENTS

This is it, the finale!

If you didn't know, With the Flames Catching Midnight is my favorite of all of my books, so it'll be sad to leave this world, but I've had such a great time. I hope you loved these characters and found comfort in this series!

To everyone who's been on this journey with me, from cover designer to editor to beta readers and supporters, thank you!

To my readers, thank you especially! I cannot wait to go on more adventures with you!

MEET THE AUTHOR

Nelly Alikyan is a girl from the Los Angeles Valley who's constantly on the move—from Boston to London to wherever she chooses next. She's the only reader in her family—not her only cause as the black sheep—and has dreamt of being a writer for as long as she can remember.

For more books and updates:
www.nellyalikyan.com